The Mark

The Mark

Bitan Chakraborty

Translated from the original Bengali by
Utpal Chakraborty

SHAMBHABI

SHAMBHABI
The Third Eye Imprint

Published by Shambhabi The Third Eye Imprint
A 10/1, Amrabati, Sodepur, Kolkata 110

Email thethirdeyeimprint@gmail.com
Website www.hawakal.com

First edition February, 2020

Copyright © Shambhabi 2020

Cover photography: Shutterstock
Cover design: Bitan Chakraborty

ISBN: 978-93-87883-87-1

Price: 300 INR | 11.99 USD

The author and the translator dedicate this collection
to
Ruskin Bond,
the celebrated connoisseur of storytelling.

Stranger than Fiction

The first man of letters in American history is recognized as Washington Irving. His short stories are iconic and continue to richly inspire new generations. "Rip Van Winkle," his most notable short story, is based on German folklore. What can we say about these stories of diffidence, transgression, human folly and resolution presented by Bitan Chakraborty?

Chakraborty's stories embody a distinct style in contemporary letters. In "Glare" the overbearing presence of modern culture overrides a personal emergency. We understand as readers that the irony suggests an overwhelming contemporary civilization doesn't value life. How does this moral situate itself in the history of short fiction?

Irving's "Rip Van Winkle" reflects feelings of uncertainty as America was beginning its trailblazing spirit of freedom in rebellion against King George III. Van Winkle wakes up after twenty years having missed the American Revolution. The story reflects the sudden social transition of the American experiment. This story was published in 1819 and neatly reflects the sentiments of post-colonial Americans. The sudden shift of milieu in combination with the uncertain future is a psychological theme within this characteristic folktale. It is the dignified position of the storyteller to invoke feelings of fear, alienation, hope, and possibility in the reader.

Short fiction is between 1,500 to 30,000 words according to *Writer's Digest*. How does the storyteller invoke our sense of wonder in such short literature?

The most emotionally relatable story in this collection is "Incompleteness." We observe a man who has an inborn disability while he struggles with relationships and his sense of self. His physical disadvantage leads him down a spiral of hopelessness and fear until he caves in to an innate weakness. The weakness becomes his strength in the long run when he is faced with another person who is disadvantaged. They meet in the strangest of places and relate in the strangest of ways. We are reminded of life's ever-present way of compensation. We don't always get what we want in life, but if we are patient life unfolds for us delicately. Experience itself is fiction, but fiction is a shared experience.

After the Transcendentalist movement of the 19th century, writers such as Jack London wrote on themes concerning the human struggle with Nature. The predominant faith of Americans is the possibility of change—including the change in character of bad people, or the need for democratic adjustment to new understandings of life. Short fiction moralizes, but its moralizing is its trust in the ability to be relevant socially. Literature must adapt to new currents in consciousness while balancing it with a sense of purpose. In the story "You and I" the storyteller's imagination invents from a common predicament. Again, as the story unfolds life's sense of purpose meets the reader unexpectedly.

Literature broadens awareness of our inner sensibilities and places its trust in the developing human being. John Steinbeck speaks of literature's moral resolutions in his Nobel banquet speech, "Furthermore, the writer is delegated to declare and to celebrate man's proven capacity for greatness of heart and spirit—for gallantry in defeat—for courage, compassion and love. In the endless war against weakness and despair, these are the bright rally-flags of hope and of emulation." Steinbeck's own short novel *Of Mice and Men* displays the gallantry of defeat when George is forced to murder his friend, Lennie, in order to protect him from a misguided mob. Steinbeck's central characters are often migrants and the impoverished: people whose lives fade from social recognition but often find a place in literature because of their grit, courage, and shortcomings. In "Lost" the characters face difficult circumstances and unveil their truth together. The story opens the collection with an energy and fear that takes us forward emotionally while uncloaking values.

In "Broken Moon" the symbolism engages the reader in a careful, but deliberate way. Note how the story begins and ends with the same situation, and as we read further the nature of the opening scene is made apparent. This story has the most vivid and tricky storytelling patterns in the collection. However, it also seems to be the most loyal to the philosophy.

Chakraborty is in defiance of the postmodern tropes that rule conventional storytelling in contemporary fiction. The brilliance of his storytelling is he does not defy deconstruction, but rather elaborates on it thematically. The story begins and ends on the same note, with the same trouble. Yet the full picture does not emerge until we endure the story with the characters. We become participants or observers of the action as we pick through its details. Chakraborty is not reacting against postmodern philosophy—instead, he is revealing a visionary approach to solving the impasse of the narrator by letting the story tell *itself* as well as inviting the reader's surprise. "Broken Moon" suggests the piecemeal nature of post-truth, but is the moon broken or is the earth broken? The moon is a piece of the earth originally. The beginning is in fact the end as well. Postmodernism neglects time and place for voice. Chakraborty demonstrates in this collection of suave realist juxtapositions that reality is independent of the narrator—of voice! Time is outside us, beyond us. Not only time, but the importance of sequence and effect.

This is an approximation of the death punch to postmodernism symbolic silence on reality and truth.

Sometimes literature speaks of higher values than our most hedonistic selves recognize. For instance, the masterful storyteller O. Henry provides us with a finely crafted parable in "The Gift of the Magi." The story captivates for its miraculous ability to hang on the edge of doom while balancing truth and the integrity of love throughout. O. Henry is often praised for his sudden unexpected plot shifts. Such element of surprise endorses the fickleness of the human predicament. They also make the reading of his stories thrilling.

Chakraborty's stories also have their uniquely crafted style. They create microcosms within microcosms—as if each twist runs parallel to the opening—like planets revolving around the sun by the law of gravity. Chakraborty's staccato sentence structure generates a unique sequence of emotion and perception of time. Fiction should not be taught to run circles around meaning while developing systemic paralysis. Each move forward should bring the reader to the edge of time into a dimension of truth and struggle.

Katherine Anne Porter, acclaimed and prize-winning fiction author, said of the story, "A story is like something you wind out of yourself. Like a spider, it is a web you weave, and you love your story like a child." Stories struggle within themselves to be born. The development of tension within the plot relies on the displacement of doubt and Becoming. The leap of faith occurs after faith is placed in suspension. Soren Kierkegaard writes in his *Journals*, "The truth is a trap: you cannot get it without it getting you; you cannot get the truth by capturing it, only by its capturing you." However, does literature perhaps have a higher responsibility than presenting the reader with truth? The careful craftsmanship of the stories in this collection reminds us that truth is indeed stranger, and more painstakingly revelatory, than fiction.

Considering the long history of science fiction, horror, and other short story genres that present readers with high imagination and suspension of disbelief it can be assumed that logic is twisted, invented, and shorn of its pride in reason within the greatest tales of fiction. Take H. P. Lovecraft as an example. Lovecraft writes in "Notes on Writing Weird Fiction," that "A certain atmosphere of breathless and unexplainable dread of outer, unknown forces must be present; and there must be a hint, expressed with a seriousness and portentousness becoming its subject, of that most terrible conception of the human brain—a malign and particular suspension or defeat of those fixed laws of Nature which are our only safeguard against the assaults of chaos and the daemons of unplumbed space." Naturally there is terror at realizing one is not in control of the life one is living.

By defining our most demanding fears and hopes, literature creates new worlds and addresses us with the humanity we neglect. Chakraborty's stories contribute to the spirited framework of short fiction in English. This edition of his stories is the present moment manifest. We face our conflicts, dreams, and denials through Chakraborty's intriguing characters. *The Mark* is part of a continuum that challenges our absurdities and humanity without partaking in judgments. To display reality without figuration or pretense is a noble achievement.

Dustin Pickering
Editor-in-Chief, *Harbinger Asylum*
24th of December, 2019
Houston, Texas

Translator's Note

Almost a year ago I had a long discussion with Kiriti Sengupta, a poet, translator and the face of Shambhabi Imprint, which is based in Calcutta. We talked about the scope of translations of Indian texts into English. From the discussion it was obvious that Bengali literature has not been translated enough and that the English-speaking world is in the dark about both old and contemporary trends in Bengali literature. I expressed my interest in translations and it was only then I came upon Bitan Chakraborty's critically acclaimed collection of Bengali short fiction, *Chinha*. I wanted to translate the stories; the most important reason behind selecting this author was I could ask him directly for clarifications when required. I picked the book up from display and went straight to page 69 to read the title story, "Chinha." In the very first page the mention of

Na*kaka*'s ghost and the description of certain footprints made me curious. I was looking forward to reading a suspense thriller. But as I progressed and met a subplot, I understood it was going to be something else. After reading the first three pages of the story I stumbled over and fumbled for the link with the preceding paragraphs. I lost interest and told the publisher about it. Sengupta, after having put on a soft smile, advised me to take the book home for my patient reading. I took it along and kept the book on the shelf for the next two months. And finally, during a quick trip to Puri I started reading the story again. As I approached the concluding paragraph, my curiosity intensified, and I tried to connect the subplots to the main story. The question arose: Whose footprints surfaced and why? I read the story again and kept on guessing. I indeed rejoiced in the process of understanding the symbolic meaning of the word, "Chinha" (The Mark). I promptly decided to read the other stories of the book, and it took a clean six days to finish off the rest. After reading the whole book I realized that the collection has several messages to convey and a proper English translation could deliver them to all corners of the world. Besides, I always felt that through translations one could meet the inner self of the author and get the scope to re-create a text which would look like an independent creation. Hence, I fell to rendering all of the stories into English. I used to carry the book to my workplace every day.

While reading the book I fell in love with it for reasons more than one. The most interesting aspect of Chakraborty's stories is his narrative style which is really off-tangent and so-far-unseen in contemporary Bengali fiction. Some flash-backs and flash-forwards have been intertwined with the present in a way that it sometimes becomes difficult to tell the narrative voice from the now silent and now eloquent expressions of the characters. Chakraborty's mastery in weaving of different tenses in the same story deserves mention.

Another important characteristic of his style is his precise and brief statements expressed through short-lived sentences. Unlike the traditional mode of story-telling, Chakraborty doesn't indulge in descriptions or elaborations of a point. His thoughts are condensed in almost each word. There is not a glide from one point to the other. There's rather a jerk in every paragraph which barely allows readers to finish off a story in one go. Each of the stories appears like a meandering river flowing slowly with many a soft murmur that speaks of the resentment, the wants and the frozen cries of the unfortunate majority. In a word, each of the stories is many micro-fictions in disguise.

Like poetry Chakraborty's short stories arrest our pace and make us think twice before moving on. What Bacon did in prose, Chakraborty seems to have done in his short fiction. Like Katherine Mansfield, he has focused attention on dropping little stones in a river continually, resulting in several forms of waves at a time, and only meditative readers see their reflections in their heart of hearts.

Lali and Fatik, two slum dwellers in "Lost," Bubu*masi*, the domestic help in "Broken Moon," Sukanta, the son of a Toto driver in "The Mark," Swapna, a harlot who suffered from breast cancer, and is now a figure for fun in "Incompleteness," are all the pillars of modern civilization but little does the society take stock of that. Chakraborty presents this rude reality of life with almost photographic exactitude. Through his amazing representation of the unclear footprints on the cement floor in "The Mark" he symbolically suggests that the Taj Mahal was not built by Shah Jahan. It was but built by those whose names weren't recorded in history. The Nobel laureate does never tell the contribution of a sweeper or a lab assistant whose help or common observations might have sparked his thought to bank upon. The father in "Glare" tells his innocent child rightly that since there is little light in human minds, people seek the outward glare of the world. Thus, Chakraborty does not go byways and hedges to have his say. He has the guts to call a spade a spade. To quote briefly the observation of celebrated Bengali poet Bibhas Roy Chowdhury, "Bitan writes directly from his experiences and not from listening to others."

Some of Chakraborty's symbols are eye-openers and heart-rending. It is through symbols that the storyteller wants to convey certain important messages: when the unclear footprints in "The Mark" become the symbol of unrecorded contributions of the working class people, multiple scratches on the old white ambassador in "Glare" become the symbol of sufferings of the innocent as well as torture of the powerful. A crutch in "Incompleteness" becomes synonymous with the incompleteness of a man. "Broken Moon" stands for the darkness of the world—abolition of dreams of enlightened women like Pritha. The injured conscience of Bittu in "Three Coins" actually has a dig at the dishonest people of the society. The gradual disappearance of the bangles of pregnant Lali amidst heavy stomping in an overcrowded train unleashes in us a silent revolution against the unequal disbursement of wealth in the society. Lali's cries become universal cries of the homeless and the deprived.

Chakraborty's use of words is simple; bulks of them are from the colloquial tongue. Since all the seven stories here have their settings in India, especially in and around Calcutta, there are a lot of Bengali words which cannot find their equals in English. For example, the use of *Nakaka, Shala, Babu, Dada,* or *Dhur* can't even accurately be expressed in any other tongue and it was indeed a challenge to catch the flavor of a Bengali dialect in a different language. Among Chakraborty's many uses of Bengali words for multiple contextual connotations, mention can be made of *Babu* and *Dada*. It's to be noted that as Bengali *Babu* can mean "Sir," it can also mean a male teacher. The use of Utpal*babu* in "Three Coins" is an instance in point. Here *babu* inspires awe. *Babu* on the other hand, can be used as a form of loving address. This use is, of course, not gender-specific. Both boys and girls can be addressed as *babu* by their parents as well as by strangers. Chhanda in "The Mark" has been addressed as *babu* by her mother. The word *Dada* (or simply, *da*) in Bengali is, however, strictly gender-specific. It is used for males only. As a form of respectful address it can be used for an older brother as well as for other older males, both familiar and unfamiliar.

Here the assistance of the acclaimed poet, translator and publisher Kiriti Sengupta deserves mention. His contribution towards the meticulous and seamless editing of each of the stories can hardly be exaggerated.

The fact that Bengali literature has its own treasure house of jewels was proved by Tagore in 1913. It was his trans-creation of a few self-composed Bengali songs and poems that fetched him the Nobel Prize. After Tagore not many literary giants in Bengal went on translating their texts. If properly translated, an array of Nobel Prizes could be bagged by Bengal, not to speak of Indian writers in English who have already proved that Indian literature has the profundity, the food for thoughts which have contributed enormously to world literature. It's a pity that great litterateurs like Shrishendu Mukhopadhyaya, Sunil Gangopadhyaya, Ashapurna Devi, Jibanananda Das, to name a few have not been translated enough. There are lots of contemporary Bengali texts of fiction, nonfiction, drama and poetry which have epical dimensions. Bitan Chakraborty's *The Mark* is one such collection that speaks of the sufferings of the deprived and the malpractices of the influential. His work awakens our morality by reflecting on certain basic values of life. His stories are protests against the injustices meted out to the weaker sections of the society. These messages need to reach every corner of the world, and Chakraborty's stories call for a concerted attempt of the world to protest against all the modern ills of the society.

Utpal Chakraborty
28 October 2019
Dum Dum, Calcutta

Contents

LOST

The black smoke climbs up. After soaring high for some time, it disperses. But since the wind is not strong, the smoke leaves a grey layer in the air after suddenly scaling high.

After persisting for a long time, Lali's pain is slowly ebbing. But now the pain lingers without even a short spell of relief. Leaning on the wall of the shoe factory for a moment, she tries to get some sort of comfort. At times the little angel kicks her in such a way that Lali is writhing in pain.

At a distance Fatik is trying to save some domestic goods from the flattened house. And some hired government officials assemble broken bamboos and mats on the fire. The more they pile dry bamboos on it the more the fire spreads its wings.

At a further distance a crowd of some overly enthusiastic people congregate.

After collecting some utensils, beddings, etc., Fatik keeps them near Lali's feet. He creates a little shadow for his pregnant wife to sit in. Laying down the goods, he murmurs, "Had I got one more hand, I could have finished the work faster."

"Is the pain too much? Bear it for a little longer, please. We will catch the train by noon. Hey… hello... that's mine... leave it... or I will push you all into fire."

Fatik rushes into the room. Of course, to call it a room is a stretch as there is nothing left of it. Only a few plastic bags and broken tiles lie helter-skelter on a square plot. Lali is struggling to put up with the pain. No, Fatik should not be bothered any further. She feels sleepy under the shadow. She is worried and thoughtful about the new place they are going to settle into. Of course, Fatik had said that according to Shasthi*da*, they could come back after this place calmed down again. Staying in a city meant he could find some sort of job quickly. But where's the scope of that in the interior, in the village? When the bridge is built here, Fatik wishes to set up a small stall for selling meat in the evening.

He sometimes says to Lali in a tone of affection, "If we sell the meat you cook, I think not a single guy in this area could avoid being your customer."

And Lali too says with puckish delight, "No, no, I can't do that. I will teach you the recipe and you will make it for your customers." After laughing a bit Fatik lies down and looks at the shed blankly.

But Lali does not believe that they would come back here again. A while ago Hema came to meet her and said, "Sister, this time I couldn't see your son's face. If luck favors, I must see your kid elsewhere. Won't you come back again?"

"It seems this time they won't allow us to be here. The officers said that after the construction of the bridge a marketplace would grow underneath."

Even as Fatik heard it he became silent. He only said, "But Shasthi*da* said that they would allow us to be there."

Lali said, "I don't know if they would let us install a small shop here on request. Then again if they do, they will charge huge money."

The pain is intensifying again. Lali stamps on the ground once or twice. They leave marks in the dust. She can't make any sound through the mouth. On the other hand, Fatik gets locked in a tussle with Dulu and his people over a claim on some utensils. Dulu's mother grabs the rice pot from Lali. Lali cranes her neck forward to tell her that the pot belongs to her. But her voice is weakened by the pain so much so that her words don't reach them.

II

Having struck Lali gently with the small bag, Fatik says, "Let's go. Hasnabad local is on platform no 8. Let's go straight."

Though Lali had heard of Sealdah station, she had never seen it before. The station is so big and the crowd so thick that almost everyone tramples each other every fraction of a moment. Fatik tries to cautiously walk fast for there are Traveling Ticket Examiners (TTE) around. The only thing he wants is to somehow board the train. At this time no mobile TTE is expected. Lali cannot go as fast as Fatik. She lags behind and the end of Fatik's *gamchha* helps her keep her balance. The passengers coming from the opposite side are constantly causing a tussle. Some express their chagrin and pass abusive words. Fatik does not respond in the least. Lali's veil drops on her back. She manages the cloth that falls off her shoulder.

The train is about to leave in the next ten minutes. All the coaches are packed now. There's no room to sit down. Fatik boards one coach with Lali, trying to guess what direction they would go after descending from the train. Lali cannot stand long. She sits down at the door with her hands pressed on her belly. Fatik arranges the bags and goods around Lali. One old passenger asks, "Where do you get off?"

"Barasat."

"Then, why are you here? Get inside. And why did you get into the train when your wife is in such an advanced stage?"

"Lali, would you sit inside?" Fatik asks, leaning over Lali.

Lali refuses to move inside. She is now completely taken over by excruciating pain. She can't sit up. She feels it would be better to spread her legs. Our little angel can't stay in this bent position of the mother. Our darling wants a bigger space. But that's not possible. As time passes the crowd thickens. Besides stretching her legs, she struggles to breathe as the air too is blocked. Calling Fatik, she says in desperation, "Air...air..."

Fatik consoles, "Wait a little while longer more... just two more stations to go... after that there will be fewer passengers."

As the train starts moving, some latecomers get into the compartment at random pressing, nudging, and shoving the passengers off. Since they will go far, they push their way inside. The belongings of Fatik and his wife become a hindrance to their movement. And the consequences become severe. All the goods gathered around Lali are about to be scattered now.

"Is this supposed to be a place to sit on?" One of the passengers shouts in a tone of rebuff.

"Get up!"

Two passengers who are standing very close try to persuade him, "Please *dada*, she is pregnant!"

"Oh, what nonsense! But what about you? You aren't pregnant, are you? So you stand up or you will be thrashed at Bidhannagar or Dumdum station."

Fatik gets up immediately. Lali shudders out of fear and pain. Her breath seems to stop in this heavy crowd of people. Their only child is in her womb and is relentlessly trying to get to the world outside. The angel keeps on complaining to the mother, "I cannot be huddled in such a small dark room anymore, *Ma*." Lali groans in pain again. The passengers standing too close to her get a bit frightened.

"What happened?" Fatik asks bending and almost falling upon her, "Is it too much to bear?"

There's no air. She can't breathe properly. Her throat is getting dry. It hurts to talk.

"Wait only a few more seconds, dear. When we get there I shall take you to the hospital. Shasthi*da* has given me the address."

Lali's features seem to fade in the unbearable pain. Fatik does not understand if Lali has heard him. A while ago, in a drunken state, Fatik had seen her wriggle in pain. But he never saw Lali suffer this way. Lali would weep then. But now Fatik doesn't want her to suffer anymore. Only when he is drunk he doesn't know what happens.

He says to Lali, "I will not make you suffer anymore. But please give me a son."

Lali says in a tone of resentment, "Yes, you can, then, sit him with the drunkards."

"Not at all, damn you! I will help him be a man."

More passengers are getting into the already packed train at random. Lali is pressed heavily against the wall made up of the passengers' legs. It is more painful to take a breath. Fatik becomes restless now. He tries desperately to see the names of the stations. The passengers are getting irritated and passing different remarks:

"What are you doing? Stand still, can't you?"

"Beware *dada*, take care of your pockets. I don't trust these people. Yesterday Das*da*'s pocket was picked. There were around three hundred rupees in his wallet."

Fatik understands their words. But he can't say anything for fear of being beaten up. So he doesn't react; looking indifferent to their remarks he says to the next passenger, "Dada, please let me know when we near Barasat station."

"Wait, the train has left Cantonment station. Stand still."

Lali feels like shouting. She is beyond thirsty. She doesn't recognize the feet of Fatik among so many. Though she lifts up her face, she can't see which feet are Fatik's. This oppression of Lali is not accepted by her baby who goes on rioting in the whole belly. Lali understands that her child wants to leave this little cloistered place, to move out into the big world. The baby feels the noise of such a throng of people and perhaps, considers them as the near and dear ones. However, Lali is apprehensive that these people will endear him in future.

Fatik leans over and lets her know, "We will get off at the next station. Many more will also get off. First I shall unload the goods and then I shall take you along. Be careful." Lali musters up her strength and says to her unborn child, "Sona, one minute please!"

The train seems to have stopped. Many people are getting down quickly. Fatik becomes dumbfounded at the rush of the passengers running out the door. Their goods and bags get scattered at the very first stroke of the crowd. People are still getting down. On the other hand, those who were waiting to catch the train had started getting into the compartment. Lali tries to stand up. Fatik throws the goods out of the train. He strikes those getting off. So in a blow they push him down. How could he stand against such a huge unbearable pressure? In one blow he lands far away from the compartment. Again the compartment starts filling up. Lali crawls inside to approach the door.

"The train has started. I will get down," Lali screams. Those hanging at the gate of the running train give her a pungent rebuff. Perhaps no one can hear her.

Fatik runs to catch hold of the handle of the compartment. He fails. One person holds the handle firmly and Fatik cannot grip it. While running through the packed platform, he can see only the pair of bangles Lali wore. Fatik runs with the train desperately but can't catch the handle even after reaching the end of the platform. He is perspiring profusely. As his head leans forward, sweat rolls down to the tip of his nose. He sees the people hanging outside the gate of the running train try hard to get in. Lali's hands visible a second ago are lost amidst the formidable struggle of the jostling passengers.

INCOMPLETENESS

Bikash slowly walks towards the gate: "Excuse me, please!" Two passengers who have been standing there make a little room for him to get down from the bus. It has been waiting long at Baguiati. As the sun slips into afternoon the area here gets crowded. It's relieving that the temperature now is low and comfortable. Bikash walks on his crutch to a nearby shop. He buys a cigarette and walks a long stretch to get to the next stop. From there he will catch another bus to Narayanpur. The bus stop here is rather lonely. The sky appears to be a canopy of red Krishnachura flowers. Bikash stands staring at the tree. A gentle gale is blowing by. Waving its head in the soft afternoon breeze, the tree lowers its branches as if to caress Bikash. He lights the cigarette and starts smoking. But hardly has he had a few drags, when he sees a bus approach. Stamping the half- finished cigarette with the buffered tip of his crutch, he gets into the bus.

Almost unmindfully he comes to stand in front of the seats, reserved for the handicapped. A young man has occupied one of them. Hinting toward Bikash, the conductor makes certain signs to request him to leave the seat. Bikash is used to such gestures. He feels reluctant to say anything about it. Without sitting there, of course, he stands brooding over his ill fate. He wonders how despite being completely normal he has to live with the permanent tag, "Handicapped." He can't make out why people consider him incomplete only because he was born with a leg that is a bit shorter than the other. Should people be judged by appearances only?

II

Bikash wants to prove himself. He is desperate. He must convince Manisha that he is not incomplete at all. Taking out the mobile from his pocket he gives her a call.

"Hello, is Manisha at home?"

"Who is it?"

"Hello, Manisha, it's Bikash."

"Right, but why are you calling? I told you not to ring my number!"

"Please, Manisha! Listen to me; I'm eager to meet you somewhere."

"Look, it's not possible for me to come unless I know how important it is to meet you."

"Please don't misunderstand me. I'm badly in need of you."

"Bikash*babu*, this is all rubbish. It's preposterous to accede to what you suggest. I can't spend my life with an incomplete person like you."

"Spardha, please!"

"Listen, I request you not to call me by that name again."

"Trust me I'm not mentally incomplete," Bikash pleads.

Spardha promptly responds, "Bikash*babu*, life doesn't thrive only with the complacency of the mind. And if you want my suggestion, I will ask you to marry a woman who is as sick as you."

Personality begets resolution, Bikash firmly believes. This notion has only grown stronger after having been with Manisha for some time. Finding things difficult, Bikash ends the conversation.

III

From Narayanpur, it is about twenty minutes' walk to Pradyut's house. Transfers are available but Bikash prefers walking all the way today.

The doorbell sounds grave in such a big house. Bikash has stayed several days here. In the moonlit night the three-storey apartment looks mysterious and the atmosphere inside the house turns eerie. Pradyut's mother lives on the first floor with all her belongings. The rest of the house is mostly vacant, aloof and submerged in darkness.

Loneliness for an indefinite time has made both the dwellers dumb.

"Ah! Bikash!" Pradyut has a British accent, "Come in, man! How did you get here? Did you hire a rickshaw or what?

"No, I just walked all the way to your house."

"Oh! But why? You short on money?"

"I enjoy strolling around, you know. Where is *masima*, by the way?"

"She is upstairs. Where else will she go?"

"I see!"

"Go to the other room, Bikash. Relax on the couch. I'll be back in a minute."

"Right, boss!"

Bikash enters a dark room. He doesn't wish to switch on the lights. He stands as if amidst the four guards of Leviathan shape all around him. These walls become fierce in his dreams. He feels like walking along a half-known, heavily congested road, where an unknown spook in the guise of a formidable creature chases him from behind. The walls with posters of upcoming cinemas on either side of the road rush forward to press him. There is no escape. No deliverance. No running away from the wrath—the animosity of the world.

"Who's there?"

Bikash gets startled by the voice of Pradyut's mother.

"I'm Bikash, *masima*."

"Oh, Bikash! Why didn't you turn on the lights?"

"I came in just now, *masima*. I was just enjoying it."

Switching on the lamps and waving the burning incenses with evening prayer song, Masima climbs up the stairs. She does not like darkness. When she sleeps, she keeps a night lamp on.

Bikash feels lifted from a helpless position. The nails and teeth of the wall have now become blunt. The walls around him seem to stand in amazement. He feels the peace and comfort of a lap. Whose lap is this? The face is incomprehensible. She can be either his *Ma* or *Masima*. But is the lap of every mother equal? Bikash, however, cannot explain Spardha's lap. It's like a lullaby that mops up all his worries and cradles him to sleep. But how strange! Just because his right leg appeared slightly shorter than the left, Spardha evaluated Bikash as incomplete, and broke off their relationship this morning!

"Would you like to have some tea, Bikash?"

Bikash wakes up to Pradyut's voice.

"Not a bad idea."

"Come to the terrace; it's windy out there."

"Okay, let's go," Bikash agrees to his proposal.

"I've got some good whisky in store; you may like it." Pradyut quips.

"But, what if *masima* comes over?"

"She won't; she is now making quilts for my children."

"What?"

"You know, *Ma* remains so worried about me these days. She wants to see me married without further delay."

Bikash is yet to finish the last peg. His stomach rolls. Lying supine on the other side Pradyut lights a cigarette and lets the smoke dribble out of his mouth. He seems to be perfectly fine.

Bikash, on the other hand, has not drunk much. Yet, he is much drowsy: "Omu, have you decided not to marry?" Omu is Pradyut's nickname; Bikash also calls him by the name when he visits Pradyut's house.

"No, I don't want to marry."

"Why?"

"I can't tell you the reason, bro. But I think, a single woman isn't enough for me."

"What do you mean, Omu?"

"Now you tell me, what is the necessity of a woman in our lives except for fulfilling our physical needs? And what is the use of a mother?"

"Listen, mothers are a class apart. Other women are like the temptation of wine. At times the addiction is strong, and at other moments it's not."

"Look Bikash, not only the women, all humans are mysterious. We all stay immersed in a bottomless ocean of light and shadow. As a result, when we see a couple, we think there is a very strong relationship between them, but by and large it is superficial. As time advances, they move far away from each other just like a flowing river widens the gap between its banks."

Bikash is visibly confused. His thoughts start breaking up at random. He shows signs of gagging. Pradyut sits up in a flash.

"Are you in a stupor?"

"Yes!"

"With these few pegs?"

"Perhaps, yes."

"What's wrong with you, Bikash?"

"Omu, I think in a relationship two complete mortal frames need to be tuned to a single rhythm."

"That's not possible, Bikash. No two persons are the same. One's rhythm never matches another's. They, however, can mingle if there are two active minds in the bodies."

"Yes, but in this regard, I think, we all are disabled."

Sensing the irony of his own words, Pradyut laughs. Bikash enjoys the cold breeze. He strikes a match which creates a temporary wound in the core of darkness. Yawning a little, Pradyut asks in a tone of half-wakefulness,

"What's happened, Bikash?"

Bikash doesn't know what to answer. Only the words of Manisha reverberate through his half-awakened sense. He feels helpless.

"Omu, do you still frequent that woman's apartment?"

"Are you talking about Mohi and Sharbari?"

"Right!"

"Not anymore."

"Why?"

"They are so boring. Playing the same old guitar is disturbing and monotonous. The bordello is a better area, rather."

"Will you take me along?"

"Shut up; don't be silly, Bikash!"

Turning to Bikash, Pradyut lights a cigarette. Then, facing the sky he lies down: "Honestly, for a few days now I feel like visiting the cathouse again. The other day I visited one. The girl was beautiful and fresh."

"Where was it?"

"It's at Bowbazar."

"Omu, I really want to go there tonight."

"Are you serious?"

"I indeed am."

"Let's go then. There are thousands of girls. We will hire a taxi, fine?"

Bikash nods.

"Think again, Bikash. Are you sure?" Pradyut wants an assurance.

"Omu, I must go. I need the proof of one truth."

IV

In the late afternoon Kolkata has seen some showers though there are no traces of rain on the other side of the city. Leaving Bikash under a tree, Pradyut slips into an alley to catch a pimp. At the slightest blow of the wind the accumulated water on the leaves starts falling. Bikash gets his hair and the back of his shirt wet. As evening sets in, this blind lane awakens. Here the nights refuse to sleep. Some women are standing at a distance; they are laughing and making fun among them. A few playful words are being addressed to the passers-by. Some respond, while some eschew. There are, of course, a few of them who notice Bikash but don't poke fun. Pradyut comes out hurriedly from inside the narrow passageway.

Almost leaning on Pradyut a hefty woman whispers in his ear, "Who is this *Kestothakur?* Where did you go, keeping him under the tree?"

Pradyut says laughing, "To fetch Radha."

"Did you get her? Or shall we find him one?"

Pradyut doesn't give any reply. Coming to Bikash he speaks in a very low voice, "Sorry, no one is free tonight."

"Nobody?"

"No."

"But the woman said that they would find me one."

"Damn them, it won't be good."

"Still, why don't you ask them once?" Bikash insists.

Pradyut thinks for a moment and says: "No, not possible today. Let's push off."

The women look at them inquisitively. One of them laughs and spits on the ground.

Pradyut asks her with much hesitation, "Is there anyone free?"

"For whom?"

"For both of us."

"One for both?"

"No, no, one for each of us."

A wave of laughter sweeps through them. Pradyut feels uneasy.

"Hey, Tepi, would you go?" One of the women asks.

"With whom?"

Pradyut points to Bikash.

"Never! I won't go to bed with a lame."

Pradyut opens his mouth to react. But Bikash handles it skilfully, "Is there anybody like me?"

"Available."

"Who's it?" asks one of the women there.

"Room No 117, up Mangala*di*'s," says Tepi.

"Who's it up at Mangala*di*'s?"

"Don't you remember Swapna, the cancer patient whose breasts were removed?" Tepi informs.

"Oh, go and show them the room, Tepi."

Meanwhile Pradyut tries to calculate the possible expenses. Bikash has never seen such narrow by-lanes before. Occasionally, his crutch hits the wall. It's impossible to walk parallel. Even within this space a group of kids hop, jump, and play. But they are not here now. Mothers are busy making business. Showing the entrance Tepi disappears with Pradyut into a different alley.

Pradyut has repeatedly warned him to avoid other pimps. Climbing the first floor one can reach room no 117 past three rooms. The number, written on the door, has blurred with time. Bikash knocks at the door twice. Nobody answers. But the light inside the room is distinctly visible. Now the knocking sounds harder. Bikash feels shy. The door opens with a screech. A short woman stands guarding the door. Taking out three hundred bucks from his pocket, Bikash offers the money to her. She lets Bikash enter the room. Bikash pretends to be jovial.

Putting the money in the pouch tucked around her waist, she says,

"If you want to eat something you have to pay, and here's a boy who will bring the food."

Standing at the doorway, the woman shouts thrice for the boy. A chap with a pale complexion comes out from a dark corner and stands before Bikash. The woman goes inside while Bikash places the order. The boy asks, "Sir, won't you booze?"

Bikash says, "No."

Eyeing him in wonder, the boy rushes out. The woman from inside insists, "Please sit on the bed." Bikash looks at the bed. It's rather clean and tidy. The spread looks new.

"Can I call you Swapna?" Bikash tries to be comfortable. The woman answers briefly, "It's okay."

"The stairs to this floor are very narrow. Don't you find it hard to climb?" Bikash inquires.

Without giving any answer, Swapna places a glass and a plate on the bed.

"I don't need a glass; I won't drink," Bikash informs once again.

Swapna removes the glass, saying, "You can have water if you feel like."

Bikash nods in agreement. The boy, after a few minutes, returns with a portion of chicken *pakoda*. He keeps the food on the table and runs out in a jiffy. The boy does not return his balance and Bikash gets puzzled. "Well, I wouldn't have taken the change. But should there be no etiquette?" He says to himself.

Arranging the plate Swapna locks the door: "Sit down, please."

Bikash sits down on the bed. Swapna sits comfortably on one corner of the bed. Bikash offers the plate to Swapna first. She refuses and returns it to Bikash.

"Won't you eat?"

"No."

"Why?"

"I'm not hungry. You eat and leave the room after doing whatever you want to do."

"Will there be more customers?"

"Yes."

"But I got the info that your business has gone down after your surgery?"

"Who told you?"

"Women downstairs."

"It's a lie."

"Well, I saw some children playing in the compound. Do you have yours among them?"

"No, I don't have any children."

"I'm sorry. Tell me something, do these children study in school?"

"Why do you need to know all such things? Would you teach them? Do whatever you have come for and leave."

While picking a *pakoda* from the plate, Bikash asks again, "How long are you in this profession?"

"Oh! You are so irritating! I'm in here for eight long years. So?"

"Will you tell me the real status of your business now?"

Leaving the bed like a burnt cat, Swapna stands up. She takes the money quickly from the pouch and pushes them into Bikash's folded palm: "Get out of my room."

Without waiting for a reply, Swapna packs up the food: "Take this along and eat them outside."

Bikash gets bewildered at the suddenness of her reaction. He stands on his crutch. "But keep these bucks. You need them."

"No, never! I don't need them at all."

"But they said that your business has lessened considerably now."

"Did you hear me? I said, get out of this room. Who told you to pity me?"

Swapna fails to control herself and tries to hide her face with her palms. Bikash readily realizes that she is weeping. He says to himself, "How could he who himself wants to be pitied take pity on you?"

While wearing shoes Bikash says, "I came here to show my virility. I wanted to prove that I'm a man and in no way an incomplete person."

"Then prove it! Why do you keep asking me irrelevant questions?" Swapna bursts out with her brimming eyes. "What will you do knowing the status of my business?"

"I know it already."

"Right. You guys know it all. You are so sure that I cannot satisfy men completely. Then, why do people come to me and ask?"

Bikash sits by the side of the bed. The bucks from his loosened fist fall on the floor. "I don't want completeness, Swapna. If you give me half, I'll fill the rest."

Can there be any definite and easy answer to this? Even if there be any, isn't that unknown to Swapna? "Is your mother alive?" asks Bikash.

Swapna nods.

"Can I put my head in your lap, Swapna?"

Swapna sits silently. Bikash starts sinking down in the void:

"Here is no cradle, not even *Masima*, who will hold my hand. Here is nothing but only drowning."

Bikash is falling down and down, without a pause, without any interruption. Gliding down from one void to another is the only truth here. All of a sudden he opens his eyes from a cold touch. He finds Swapna's soft fingers rested on his forehead.

THE MARK

Chhanda has now been entrusted with a new task. She has to clean all the dust that has heaped up over a period of fifteen years. Isn't it too much? Pampa, the domestic help, has refused to do this lately.

"Spare me, please. I'll not enter that room again. I've been working for quite some time now in your house, and so long I didn't notice any footprint of anyone on the floor," said she.

Pampa still believes that the ghost of Na*kaka* will come back, wanting to take possession of his room. For past fifteen years this room belonged to Na*kaka*. Chhanda then was in her teens and was to appear for her school leaving exam. After retiring from Islampur College, Na*kaka* came back to this house with a truck-full of books. Chhanda's father had died three years ago. Her mother felt relieved that at least one male would be there at home.

Though Nakaka was the only male member of the family, he never wanted to be their guardian. He was a man of few words and spent the days buried in books. It was only at certain times that he would call Chhanda to speak to her about different philosophies of the world. All those complex reflections did not interest her at all. Rather they appeared abstruse and far-fetched. The only thing she focused her attention on was that room. It was open on two sides. During summer gentle gale blew through the windows all night, and in the morning the sun seemed to lie almost near the legs of the plank. She too could hardly recall any visible mark on the floor of that room.

Before Nakaka came, only a thick carpet was laid on the floor, and two almirahs stood around the corner. In childhood her father used to sit on the carpet every Sunday to help Chhanda with her studies. Even then she didn't notice any footprints there. After the death of Nakaka she was allowed to use that room again.

Taking the plank out of the room, she again spread the carpet on the floor. Two extra bookshelves, one table under the right window, and an armchair were left in the room.

Pampa got the plank of Nakaka shifted to a different place. Of course, to call it a plank would be a misnomer because it's as low and as simple as a cot. What makes it stand apart is its four wooden stands which was entirely Nakaka's improvization for hanging the mosquito net. Subhaskaka who was multi-talented, some-time technician of this house, lived in a slum called Sahebpara. He was always at the beck and call of Na*kaka*. No matter if the task was to make a house, or build a chair or rebuild a tulsi-podium; it was Subhas*kaka* who would collect all kinds of technicians, makers, plumbers, etc., and he himself would become their supplier. Again if the task was small, he himself would become both a laborer and a technician.

Once Subhas*kaka* was called to construct a part of the floor of the house. Upon observing the place he said,

"This is only a half-day's work, *babu*. I shall do it all myself. Please bring me five sacks of sand, three sacks of stone chips, and two bags of cement. The rest I'll manage." With these words, he squeezed his face and said,

"From now on my *didimoni* will play here. She will open a school of her own and I shall be her first student."

Chhanda leapt in an inward celestial joy. Her school friend, Mithu, had a playing room but she had none. Quite naturally, her happiness knew no bounds. Na*kaka* didn't come home that year. He didn't even visit them during the pujas.

It was Chhanda who after having moved the plank first saw the footprints on the floor. Not that the mark was very clear; there were several black spots. The impression of cement spatula was obvious. The floor had never been polished properly. Rubbing out the black marks, Pampa grunted, "Alas, the part of the floor below the plank was never mopped." One day it was Pampa who discovered that a new footprint had surfaced clearly by the side of the existing footprint. Since then she never entered this room again even by mistake.

Chhanda has set up a tutorial in this house. She takes both morning and afternoon classes. After the end of the first batch, Chhanda herself wipes the room. She swabs the footprints cautiously as she doesn't want those black spots to mar the sheen of the floor.

Tutun is Chhanda's nickname. Her father used to call her by this name. However, her mother calls her by any name convenient to her: Tutun, Buri, Sona or Chhanda. Na*kaka* used to call her by the name, Tun. Once he wrote in a letter, "I named you Tun. Two (tu) and two (tu) make four. And there remains the N of Tutun (tu+tu+n). N becomes alone, and no one will befriend the left out. So, I've removed one of the twins."

Chhanda didn't understand all this. But as time rolled by she got used to this connotation. Her uncle was as tall as her father. If anyone inquired about his height, he said, "Earlier I was 5 feet 8 inches but now I've added an inch more. Don't ask me how I managed. You know, if I had been taller by a few inches I could have been a detective. So, I kept a beard and became Plato."

After having come home permanently, he asked Chhanda's mother, "*Boudi*, does Subhas come here now?" Spitting out the spittle, she responded,

"He will come if informed. What do you want from him?"

"I'll arrange a recliner because I want to enjoy all the comfort of my retirement."

The news reached Subhas*kaka* in no time and he came home in the evening. He was coughing hard. His health didn't seem quite fine. Na*kaka* made him understand the things to be bought. Hearing all these he said with a smile, "Why would you buy what is made by a different hand? Allow me some time, I'll make it for you."

When her uncle wanted to make an advance payment, Subhas*kaka* said, "Still I have the goodwill to get credit from the shops. Let me finish the recliner first, I will then ask for a payment. Please don't worry about that."

It took him a month's time to complete it. Coming home every day, he worked on it for hours at a time. Na*kaka* used to watch the activities, which Chhanda did take stock of. This was not vigilance. Nor was it to give Subhas*kaka* directions or to find flaws in his job. He eyed all these to look for something else.

While watching him work Na*kaka* suddenly asked, "Would you tell me Tun, who built the Taj Mahal?"

"Shah Jahan," answered Chhanda, taking a morsel of puffed rice from the bowl into her mouth.

Na*kaka* replied, "What a fool you are! You didn't even listen to my question properly. Shah

Jahan paid for the mausoleum. Do you know who built it?"

"Let alone me, I doubt whether Shah Jahan himself knew it."

"Yes, yes, that's quite right!" Na*kaka* took the last sip from the cup.

The task of Subhas*kaka* was almost over. He was rubbing the polish off his hand with turpentine oil. It was too late at night. Fetching the wallet from his room, Na*kaka* made the payment.

"Subhas, could you come again tomorrow with the chisel?"

Managing the bark, Subhas*kaka* nodded, "I must come *dadababu*; I've not much work left."

While mopping up the floor today, Chhanda noticed more carefully that the footprints appeared clearer. They looked like petrified fossil. Each mark appeared more vivid. At a glance the two feet together made eight fingers. This was because both the little fingers looked so small that they seemed to be nonentities. She tried to recall the feet of Na*kaka*. They were fair but hairy. The hair was so black and shiny that they easily caught everyone's attention. Chhanda once more dipped the rag in the water and squeezed it. Every dashami she had to touch Na*kaka*'s feet as a routine task. Though she did not remember it with photographic exactitude, it could be said with emphasis that his little fingers were not, after all, pudgy.

"I don't understand why dadababu makes fun always," said Subhas*kaka* who felt too blushful at Na*kaka*'s remark. He put the chisel back in the bag. Restless Na*kaka* got up from the chair and urged, "Subhas, what's the harm in it? Why will the chair be my own?"

Subhas*kaka* hugged him with his two hands and said, "Please *dadababu*, don't make me feel shy anymore."

In the meantime Chhanda's mother came to the porch. Na*kaka* kept his hands on the shoulder of Subhas*kaka* and said, "If I knew how to use the chisel, I could have done it myself, Subhas. This is my request. Please follow my words."

"*Dadababu*, you have always appreciated my work heartily. If you insist, I'll sit on the chair someday. But please don't ask me to do this."

"What happened again?" without understanding what was going on, Chhanda's mother inquired.

"Ask *dadababu*, please. He has lost it!" lifting his blushful face Subhas*kaka* uttered those words laughingly.

"Subhas, hand the chisel to me. I'll do it myself," Na*kaka* looked determined. Subhas*kaka* couldn't refuse anymore. He pushed the bag forward. Na*kaka* took the chisel out of the bag.

Chhanda opened the envelopes that contained the fees given by her students. She had to note the names and make a list of the students who had paid up. It was the 10th day of the month; a batch of twelve students. However, only seven of them had paid the money. Though the fee was as low as five hundred rupees, the students were indifferent toward paying their tutor. Had Chhanda charged fifteen hundred bucks like GKS Sir, the condition of the students would have been worse.

In the evening batch, Chhanda must rebuke them for not paying fees on time. Only two of them cleared their dues last week. This should not continue forever. Chhanda's eyes got stuck on the name of Sukanta Maity on the list.

The boy hadn't come for past five weeks. He lives in Sahebpara. A bit skinny, he comes from a needy family. His father drives auto rickshaw. Sukanta is timid by nature. Perhaps, he does not know how to laugh out loud. He laughs hiding his mouth on his chest. It doesn't make any sound. Each time he pays the tuition fee there are small currency notes inside the envelope. In the beginning Chhanda used to be surprised at this. However, this helped Chhanda with her payments for daily chores.

"Why isn't he attending the classes? I've to find it out on Wednesday," Chhanda muttered.

"*Babu*, would you come here for a minute?" Chhanda's mother has come up to clean the room of Na*kaka*. Pujas are ahead. The rooms need to be cleaned.

"What happened?"

"Take that chair outside. Its legs are covered in soot."

Chhanda pulls the chair out. Na*kaka* would always put a thick cloth on the seat before using the chair. Chhanda and her family maintain the spread even now. But they don't wash it regularly.

Today the cloth will be dipped in detergent. Chhanda dusts the chair with a dry rag. How sooty it is, indeed! The polish now shines glaringly. As she starts cleaning it with a wet rag, the letter "S" near the right leg catches her eye. "S" has been written with a number of straight lines.

"Abhirup, any idea about why Sukanta doesn't come nowadays?"

"Don't you know Miss, Sukanta's father met with an accident a few weeks ago? One truck rammed into the back of his vehicle."

"What! Wasn't his father an auto driver?"

"Yes, he was one. But he doesn't drive the auto-rickshaw anymore. It's been almost a year that he has bought a Toto."

"How is he doing now?"

"He has been discharged from the hospital. But he cannot walk. This year Sukanta may not appear for the school exam. His father took a loan from a bank and they have to repay the debt."

"What is Sukanta doing now?"

"He has repaired the Toto and is driving it himself."

Chhanda got distracted. She seemed to be transported into a different world. Meanwhile, all the students packed up and left slowly.

"Tell me one thing, Na*kaka*. You wrote the initial of Subhas*kaka*'s name on the chair, but does it entitle the chair to him?"

"No, not at all."

"Then why did you create a noise around it in the evening?" Chhanda, thus, tried to prank Na*kaka* during his dinner.

What an eating habit! Although the mother and her daughter will eat rice at night, Na*kaka* will take milk with puffed rice. He avoids heavy meals at night; Na*kaka* believes he won't sleep properly if he gorges on heavy food.

"You are right, *thakurpo*! What you did in the evening was superb," says Chhanda's mother.

Na*kaka* addressed it laughingly, "Had Subhas not insisted, you could not have known the matter. Again, what is there to be known in this? But Tun, do you know that possessiveness makes one too miserly?"

"But you didn't answer my question," Chhanda responded with a smile.

"I was about to answer you. Possessiveness! See, how a man safeguards what belongs to nature by fencing it and claims it to be his own. And then, one more powerful man comes and declares that it is he who is the owner of all of these. A kingdom is formed and a potentate comes to reign supreme. On the contrary, those who really work for the people in the kingdom become stupid sycophants of the ruler. History gloriously records the names of the kings, whereas the real architects of civilization live on forgotten and ignored."

While collecting used dishes and leftovers Chhanda interrupted Na*kaka*, "This is the rule of the world! He who invents becomes the owner of his invention. If one goes by your theory, then for each discovery, the lab assistant, even the sweeper of the laboratory should be taken into account. If the Nobel Prize is to be offered, it is to be awarded to the lab assistants as well as sweepers of the laboratories."

Na*kaka* leaned on the chair. He was chewing a piece of dry *haritaki*, "Man gets the Nobel for intelligence. But in order to implement talent the help of other people is undeniable."

Drying her freshly washed hand with her scarf, Chhanda hung the mosquito net for him.

"Relax, Na*kaka*! I can tell you that your thoughts are not logical and this is why Philosophy has been a part of humanities."

Tomorrow Pampa won't come. One of her sisters is getting married. No point in dumping the used dishes. Chhanda's mother isn't keeping well. After washing plates in the kitchen, Chhanda comes to switch on the table lamp in Na*kaka*'s room. Higher Secondary exam is ahead. Mock tests are to be arranged for her students. Question papers have to be set. Chhanda has bought the table lamp online. It looks classy. She remembers long ago she saw such a lamp in Satyajit Roy's room, as published in a magazine.

Chhanda sits down with papers. Pratik Roy has scored the highest marks this year as well. He is meritorious but seems extremely reserved like the ancient ants on the earth. Pratik comes to tuition, collects notes meticulously; it looks like he is preparing for hibernation. His father comes to take him home regularly and inquires, "I hope you aren't forgetting anything, are you?" And then he turns to Chhanda to ask, "Could you finalize the dates for the mock test?" Please let me know well in advance. I want Pratik to appear for more such exams at other centers. I hope the dates don't clash." Chhanda is sure that Pratik will leave his mark in the upcoming exam.

After a long time Somlata, Na*kaka*'s attendant, came today. When he was bedridden, finding an attendant was difficult. It was Subhas*kaka* who helped them find Somlata. She worked from 9 am until 9 pm, for a stretch of twelve hours a day. Somlata served for one and a half year.

Chhanda's mother is cutting vegetables as she sits on the verandah. Chhanda is making tea. Somlata enters Na*kaka*'s room and looks around. She says with a sigh: "He was a genuinely good human being!"

While saying this her voice shivers, and at the same time, Chhanda's mother wipes her moist eyes with the fag end of her sari. Chhanda looks frequently at the wall clock.

Today the results of the Higher Secondary examination will be declared. Chhanda expects at least four students from her class will excel this year. GKS Sir won't be happy with Chhanda's students fairing quite well, perhaps. She plans to start admission tests for students who want to enroll for tuition classes. She will teach everybody but an admission test will add seriousness to her classes, Chhanda assumes. She also plans to hike her fees. All these depend on today's results. It's 9.22 am. And the results will be available online after 10 am. She has kept the cell phone on the kitchen counter.

"Somlata, do you know Subhas' whereabouts?" Chhanda's mother inquires all of a sudden.

"Subhas*da* is no more, didn't you know?"

"What! What did you just say?"

"Subhas*da* expired about seven months ago. He was very ill and could not afford medicines. His son didn't look after him at all. Leaving his father alone he shifted to a new house after marriage."

Chhanda listens to all these with avid attention. Somlata continues, "Do you know *didi*, during Subhas*da*'s last few months he kept complaining about aching toes? Those were badly eroded!"

Chhanda gets alert.

"Hello, Madhura, say your result."

Madhura shouts in excitement, "*Didi*, 87% in aggregate. I've got 83 in Biology."

All of Chhanda's students keep calling. So far twelve students have got the first division. Four have secured the star mark. Chhanda seems anxious about Pratik who is yet to call.

Madhura rings again, "*Didi*, I'm so happy; I'll see you in the evening. What about Pratik?"

"Oh! I'm yet to get his call."

"What! *Didi*, didn't you see him on the TV?"

Chhanda totters.

"What happened to him?"

"He has stood fifth in the state."

Chhanda forgets to say thanks or bye to Madhura. She rushes to grab the remote control to switch on the television. Seeing her in such a hurry, her mother asks, "What's happened?"

Chhanda quickly surfs the news channel to reach the right one. There he is.

"Look, Pratik has stood fifth in the Higher Secondary exam. You know him, *Ma*."

"Let me put my specs on first."

The anchor of the show is repeating the name of Pratik. Across the screen Pratik's face appears large. The teachers of his school are feeding him sweets…

Chhanda's dark horse has won, finally! She feels like dancing in joy.

"Did you expect this result?" The journalist forwards the mic.

"I was sure I would do well, but honestly, I didn't expect this much."

"What will you study now?"

"I'll decide once the Joint Entrance Exam results come out."

"How many hours a day did you study, by the way?"

"About five to six hours."

Pratik keeps answering like a celebrity. Chhanda's eyes moisten in joy.

"How many tutors did you have?"

"I didn't have any private tutor. My schoolteachers helped me, and at home my dad would teach."

"What a fat lie! How could Pratik say that?" Chhanda's mother says unmindfully. Chhanda stands still. She can't believe her ears. She sits on the chair next to her mother.

"He is one such guy who drinks milk but blames the milkman," Somlata picks up her bag. "I'll now leave, *didi*," she tells Chhanda's mother.

Chhanda does not look at Somlata. Did Somlata smile? Chhanda thinks so.

From early evening the students came to show their score sheets. Chhanda was nice to all of them. She gave them advices for future studies. But she hadn't eaten anything since afternoon. Chhanda's mother tried to convince her daughter; she told her to drop the matter and forget the entire incident. Chhanda refused to follow and eat. She sat on the recliner Subhas*kaka* had made for Na*kaka*. The one line that kept ringing in her ears: "I didn't have any private tutor."

It's quite late in the night. Chhanda locks the front gate of the house and enters Na*kaka*'s room. She turns off all the lights except the table lamp. Her mother is still in the kitchen. She is, perhaps, cooking dinner. Chhanda approaches the footprints. They look sharper than before. Nine toes; only the little toe of the right limb appears merged with the foot. Several wrinkles around the heels and marks of random strokes of a spatula by an unskilled hand are visible as well. Chhanda places her right foot on the footprint and then the left foot. She pulls up the salwar to check whether her feet resemble the footprints. They look all the same. Only her little toe appears protruded. It seems with every passing moment it will get shorter, and perhaps after some time the little toe would also match the mark on the floor. And it is then that someone would suddenly ask Chhanda, "Who made the Taj Mahal, Tun?"

YOU AND I

Kolkata does not usually have summer so early. At least gusts of strong wind pay a visit in the afternoons. The nighttime doesn't seem that unbearable. But this year, there will be no respite from the sultry heat of the season. A *kalbaisakhi* is not on the cards, perhaps. During daytime the air from the ceiling fan seems to create a heat-wave in the room. Besides, due to extreme humidity the sweat fails to dry up. It's really hard to keep focus on any work in the office during this time.

In such sweltering heat of the day a young fellow is found waiting by the side of the road. Occasionally, he is checking his cell phone to know the time. He looks worried; he has smoked off two cigarettes in a short spell. This is not an uncommon scene on the lanes of Kolkata. Nevertheless, it has caught my attention today, and as I don't have much to do in the office now, I am feeling free to observe the guy. My curiosity knows no bounds. Endless questions crowd in my mind: "Is he waiting for something? Is he expected to meet a client along with his colleague? Has he failed to achieve the sales target, as set by his manager? Or, is he anticipating a golden handshake?"

From here I can see the trousers and full-sleeve shirt the guy is sporting. He is carrying a black backpack long ways. Perhaps, he doesn't intend to hold it by the hand. Does he want to hide his sweaty shirt, glued to his back? I can't see his feet clearly through the office window, for the fringe of the window ledge creates a hindrance. The guy must have worn boots, although they look like grey sports shoes from here.

"But why am I so concerned about the guy? Do I really know much about him? Why do I search for details in such a mundane scene?"

The young chap lights a cigarette again. There is frequent inhalation—interval between the puffs becomes short. With every passing second he is perhaps losing patience. Each of his drags seems stronger than before.

"Will he throw off the stub and leave? If so, the scene will die prematurely. And in such idle hours in my office, I have to wait for another show to feast upon. I should rather smoke a cigarette and continue to observe."

Treading the smoldering butt when the guy is about to walk ahead, a girl enters the scene. She is dragging him back to the previous place. Her unkempt hair can be seen from behind the umbrella. The long tresses bounce on her waist with every step.

"But, who is this fairy? How has she stopped the untimely death of the scene? Oh goddess of disheveled hair! Let me kiss you."

"Oh Gawd, what did I just say? Should I kiss a woman like this? This is exactly why people say, *an idle mind is the devil's workshop.*"

My cigarette burns and I keep watching the scene. The guy's face isn't visible anymore. It is covered by the umbrella.

One unknowingly becomes conscious in excitement. The girl folds down her umbrella. It's a pain to have a showdown with the umbrella open. A few people, walking down the road, look at them. The hands and lips of the girl are quivering in a dramatic mode. The guy keeps mum. It seems he has nothing to say. Has he fallen short of arguments? The whole world perhaps stands claiming an answer and the chap fumbles in vain. Probably, he is trying hard to prove his helplessness.

"Am I being partial to the guy?"

In fact, sitting in my office I can't see anything more than the vigorous shaking of the girl's head and the fierce movement of her hands. Not a single word reaches me from her mouth. So chances are fairly high that my thoughts are turning lopsided.

Just now I have caught a glimpse of her eyes. The girl has turned her face around to wipe off the tears. As if, she does not want the guy to have the least trace of her sorrow. The boy brings his hanky out of his pocket and offers it to her. The girl throws it away on the road. She doesn't need one. Her *dupatta* can hide her kohl-hued tears. The girl does not wait anymore but looks at the guy one last time.

"O' Lord, what a sight! You allowed me to witness those eyes— eyes as perplexing as that of Yashodhara whom Siddartha failed to address as he was about to leave the Lumbini palace."

The sun has paled. The ashtray too has become full. There is absolutely no work to be done in the office. As I close the window of my cabin, I look at the footpath below only to find it turning into a smoking zone of the tired afternoon walkers.

"How about going to a teashop?"

A cup of tea and then, wait for the train. Fried peanuts will be sold by hawkers inside the compartments. By the way, will the boy buy them today? Will the girl, though disturbed, eat *fuchkas* while she accompanies her maternal aunt for the evening stroll? Whatever it is, the whole world will not care a damn. Will it bother the man who stands by my side every day in the bus? Like every other day he too will enjoy a nap, standing. As I approach the teashop I see a short instruction: *Please use the bin.*

A tin drum used as a dustbin is only a few meters away. As soon as leftovers and used clay cups are thrown in it, some flies perching about seem to get annoyed and express their dislike. There's a park close by: people starting from the teens to senior citizens have thronged there. Many of them will be sitting in the park until late evening. There is no room left except the last bench. I see that guy with a morose look is sitting on it. He has kept the backpack aside. Just now, two loafers arrive to have tea. They are speaking foul words on something, it seems. A bit irritated, the teashop owner asks, "How many of you want tea?"

"Three," another boy joins the gang and starts talking rubbish. Do they have any amount of empathy for that guy who is visibly sad? Who knows what will happen to him! He may stand under the shower a long time while he returns home, and the tea, served by his ma, may turn cold. As the group of loafers lurch violently in laughter, the clay cups start spilling over.

I didn't feel like battling with the crowd in the train and opted for a bus instead as I left the teashop.

Did anyone notice that I boarded the bus at Sukiya Street stop? Other passengers look quite stern. Most of them seem to be mourning personal losses. Am I a ghost or what! The man by whose side I sit does not seem happy about my presence and shifts slightly on the other side to allow me space. He's the one to have proven that I am alive.

I turn around to find everybody is on tenterhooks for something unknown to happen. Their faces become grimmer at every signal the bus stops. I'm enjoying the overall ambience. As the bus halts at Fariapukur I shift towards the window. The burning bitumen of the road fumes hot air every moment. Is that guy exhaling the same? Did that girl, after getting fresh, check the list of dialed numbers on her cell phone?

It took thirty minutes to cross Shyambazar area. Bagbazar Bata is thickly crowded. There is the mad rush of buyers for the *chaitra* sale.

Suddenly, I find an octogenarian extending his hand towards me. With a lozenge clutched between his fingers he says endearingly, "Hello brother, take this candy please." As I get it, he offers candies to other passengers. Sitting on the same seat he reaches out to as many passengers as possible by extending his hand in several directions. The depressed faces brighten. "Why this candy, all of a sudden!" No one could actually ask. I look at the old man again, this time with wide eyes. He has wrinkled skin, edentulous jaws, and a smudged mark of vermillion on his forehead. His tucked up shirt with hints of green, looks worn out. From inside the tattered bag he is carrying on his shoulder a packet of candies is peeping out. At every stop his hand reaches out to whoever is boarding the vehicle. The passengers laugh by getting over their ego.

Cool breeze is, finally, circulating inside. I'm to get down. Addressing the old man by *dadu* and thanking him from my heart I get off the bus with the aroma of the sweet green mango candy sticking to my palm. As I breathe in the smell again, I remember the good old childhood days. My eyes moisten. All my frustrations vanish immediately. Had that guy not been late, he too would have availed this bus. Couldn't the whiff of the sweet candy have washed away a bit of his sadness?

GLARE

A white old ambassador car is waiting long on the narrow lane. It has blocked the way, causing much hindrance to the traffic flow. Several scratch marks are visible all over the body of the car. The mirror on the left side is covered by a piece of red *salu*. And the right mirror shows multiple cracks. Craning his neck outside, the driver appeals,

"*Dada*, we got a patient; please allow us to pass."

"Shut up, stupid! Can't you hear? Your car won't move an inch ahead," Nantu strikes the bonnet repeatedly. Facing the lengthy hold-up due to road closure and getting no space on the jam-packed narrow lane, Pradip with his kid finds it safe to stand by the side of the drain. Pradip peeps through the car window—a frail man is lying on the seat with his head rested on a woman's lap. He remains still. Following his father, Mainak insists, "What are you looking at, *Baba*? I also want to see."

Meanwhile the announcement begins, "And now the stage will be graced by..."

Pradip left his office early this noon. He should be at home with a half-pound ordinary fruit cake. Mainak won't eat any other cake. Wood apple jam, stuffed in such cakes, is irresistible to him. Other cakes are too costly to afford, and Mainak never had a chance to savor them either.

During this time various kinds of fruit cakes, wrapped in bright papers, are sold at every counter. Ordinary fruit cakes are cheap—fifty-five bucks a piece. Yet, Pradip had to seek help from his office colleague, or else he would have nothing left in his pocket for the New Year's Eve. 250 grams of chicken, 500 grams of potatoes, ginger of 10 rupees, 200 grams of onion, 25 grams of garlic and 200 grams of tomatoes will cost more than one hundred rupees: Pradip has planned a chicken meal for his family on 31st evening. Today there will be a big cultural event in the locality: the best performers from the reality shows are being fetched for the event. Arrays of large loudspeakers have been set on the trees and lampposts in the vicinity. Pradip has promised to take Mainak to the venue. The programme is expected to begin at 7 pm sharp.

Half-an-hour before the scheduled time the Suri playground is full and the crowd has extended up to the point where the car is stranded. It's rather a narrow link road to the highway. This short-cut is preferred by many drivers to save on time. But today there's no chance of availing this road. Mainak is eager to see Khokon Shau sing and snap a photo with his father's mobile. He has been the winner of the season. After finishing his homework Mainak watches the talent hunt programmes on television everyday with his mother. This is why the names of all participating singers are at his fingertips.

Owing to the huge crowd Mainak fails to see anything from below, he grizzles. The intermittent honk along with the blare from the loudspeakers is producing a cacophony. Mainak can't hear properly. Pradip puts Mainak on his shoulder to help him view the performance.

Nowadays small cars including ambulances navigate through this lane to reach the main road. But nowhere on the lane is placed a warning: road closed. So only after approaching a long way drivers get to know of the closure. Since the lane today is blocked by bamboo staves, no car can actually pass. The ambassador car has to leave immediately and turn back a long stretch to get to the previous road. But the driver doesn't want to understand this. He keeps on requesting fervently, "Please allow us to move ahead; it's a serious case. Reversing the direction won't help, the patient will die on the way."

Nantu is looking after this side of the road today. He will not budge an inch. The buck of keeping the honor of the area has fallen, as if, on his shoulder. When Pradip came to live in a rented house in this area, Nantu was in school. He gave up his studies thereafter. However, it was Nantu who did all co-curricular activities for the school: be it the *Saraswati Puja* or *Rabindrajayanti* he had the last word on every occasion. He has even had a strange command over the proceedings of the polling station. From dawn to dusk he remains more active than the central force posted outside the polling booth. Though he is quite young, some 20 plus, Nantu has such a chequered experience of rigging that Pradip fails to understand even at his age.

Such an annual function is celebrated here with much razzmatazz. The famous singer Kumar Sanu performed last year. And this is the one day when no car is permitted to pass across this lane.

"Why damn it, didn't you hear the sound from the loudspeakers as you drove in? Go back, I'm telling you. If my folks gather around, you will see the worst." While saying these, Nantu loses his balance and falls on Pradip.

"*Baba*, what perfume has Nantu*da* used? He smells so bad!"—Mainak hides his nose between his palms. This technique he has mastered from his mother.

The driver finds no space to turn the car around. He is left with no choice but to drive in reverse through the thick crowd. Considering it very intimidating as well as time-killing, he requests one last time, "*Dada*, please consider; the patient may die." Nantu feels much annoyed and turns furious—"Hey Kelo, come to this side. Here is a damn stupid driver who needs to be thrashed. He can't follow my simple instructions." A plump boy comes forward shoving off the bamboo barrier. Pradip doesn't know whether he is Kelo. The other day this guy was seen sitting near the bus stop and coercing *puja* subscriptions from the truck drivers. Along with his gang he was also seen outside the booth on poll days. Dressed in traditional attire they threatened the voters.

"Listen piglet, can't you see a function is going on here? Turn back right now. Hurry up!"— Kelo snarls.

"*Dada*, here's a patient. Just allow us to pass this time only. Taking another route will delay his admission to the hospital and he will invariably die," the driver beseeches his grace.

"See, a single word further will land you in hell. Got it? Drive back right now." Kelo blows hard on the bonnet. Being spurred, Nantu also slaps the windshield. The car shakes vigorously. Kelo picks up a broken brick bar, aims it at the car, starts shouting curses and directs the driver in a commanding tone, "Move, move, move back now!"

Pradip notices that the fragile man, lying in the car, stirs up. One motorbike that also braked behind the car steered back and fled off, dozing through the pedestrians and onlookers. Khokon Shau is now on stage. Many more spectators have gathered. Their eyes can't stand the glaring lights put up on stage. Nothing is distinctly visible on the dais. The songs from the loudspeakers sound harsh. Riding his father's shoulders Mainak stretches his neck to check on Khokon Shau. But he fails to see anyone on stage. He is sad that his *Baba* does not own a quality smartphone. Mainak clicks the mobile camera a few times only to get blurred images.

It's very cold today. Mist is enveloping the surroundings by and by. Pradip gets his hair wet. Sumi has been ringing him repeatedly, "Pradip, bring Babai back home or he may catch cold."

The tune of the popular lyric, *tujhpe tiki hain meri naughty najaria* (*my naughty eyes rest on you*), is gradually dying out in the thick wind. The organizers have had this part of the locality bedecked with numerous rice lights. Dolled up in colorful strings, the entire stretch has taken on a gorgeous look of celebration. A small pack of spicy puffed rice has almost compensated Mainak's grief of missing a close-up view of the songster Khokon Shau: "Why do people go for such radiance on Christmas day, *Baba*? Why do they light up such an uncountable number of rice lamps on this day?" asks Mainak.

"Out of the joy of the birth of Jesus Christ, the Messiah," responds Pradip.

"Oh well, then why don't you arrange such glittering lights on my birthday?" Mainak asks again.

"Actually you were born in the morning when no star is found in the sky. Jesus was born at night, and there were the twinkling stars in the sky. This is why people prefer such dazzling lights on this occasion." Pradip concludes.

"*Baba*, can you see the stars tonight?" Gripping the packet of puffed rice tightly in his hands, Mainak looks up.

Facing the sky, Pradip suggests, "See Babai, the stars are up there."

"What's the need of so many strings then, *Baba*? Did people in Jesus' time light up so many lamps to celebrate his birth?"

Pradip laughs. He does up his son's cap and says in a candid tone, "Look Babai, stars rise up in the sky even today. But it's a pity that we don't have the right vision to see them. This is perhaps why we need such a glaring show of dazzling lights all around us."

Mainak keeps silent. Standing like a statue he seems to gobble up each of his *Baba*'s words in amazement.

THREE COINS

From the other side of the road it is clearly visible that quite a few potatoes are being boiled on a deep pan; spices mixed with oil make the soup. Ratan*da* uses a ladle to serve two small potatoes and a little gravy on a steel bowl. He then takes out the loaf from the tin box... Bittu checks on his watery mouth.

The warning bell rings to mark the end of the break. Those who were playing on the ground rushed to their classrooms. A few students studying in the upper grades, however, showed a laid back attitude. Bittu looks at Ratan*da*'s shop one last time and runs to his class. Utpal*babu* doesn't usually arrive late for his classes. He waits in the teachers' room for the final bell and keeps the whip handy. On the way to room 14 he will randomly flog the students he would get within his reach. Bittu takes out the geography book from his bag and flips through the pages. Today Utpal*babu* would ask students to draw pictures on diurnal motion. He might call the guardians of those who would fail to do so.

Bittu is relieved when Utpal*babu* asks Tanay, the first boy, to illustrate the phenomenon on the blackboard. Drawing the earth like a round potato with a yellow chalk, Tanay explains how the earth revolves ceaselessly round the sun.

While listening to him Bittu again thinks of Ratan*da*'s shop. He could envision how Ratan*da* slices the bread with a long knife... with every loaf how he improvises on the technique ... he then fills the bowls with the clear soup and sprinkles salt and pepper. Placing a spoon in each bowl, how fast Ratan*da* serves the customers from one table to the other.

Bittu's mother cooked potatoes for his last birthday. But the soup and the breads were missing. Ignoring the delectable luchi his mother made on the occasion, when he asked for breads, Bittu's father scolded him, "This isn't a healthy choice at all." Bittu's eyes welled up. His mother pulled Bittu toward her and ran fingers through his hair, "You are my good boy, aren't you? Why would you eat white bread instead of luchi on this day? Luchi is a traditional delicacy!"

Suddenly, the chalk hits Bittu's forehead with a sound. Utpal*babu* never fails to reach the target. "Stand up," says the teacher. Picking the chalk up from the floor Bittu stands upright like a statue.

Utpal*babu* asks, "Say, what is a leap year?" In such circumstances Bittu used to down his head when he was in the lower grades. He has become smarter with time. Looking briefly at the blackboard, he says unhesitatingly, "I don't know, Sir." Utpal*babu* seems angry, "Why? Where had you been for so long?" Bittu responds, "Here, Sir."

Students from the last bench try hard to control their bouts of laughter. Utpal*babu* probes further, "Since you were here, I can assume that you heard the text I taught. Why can't you answer then?" He becomes aggressive and clutches the whip. Bittu understands what is in store for him. He is scared but says politely, "Sir, I heard you, but failed to understand."

Looking at Bittu, Utpal*babu* keeps the whip on the table. Bittu keeps standing with his head down. Convinced by Bittu's frank confession Utpal*babu* asserts, "You are excused for today. You have to be attentive in the class. Sit down now."

II

On their way back home Partha takes out a gold card from his pocket. "You too can get one from the shop in exchange for ten Sandy chewing gum wrappers," Partha says.

"So how many cards did you gather until now?" inquires Joy.

"Fifty cards!" Partha responds.

Joy looks sad and says, "I've got only twenty."

Soumya adds to the conversation, "I don't think I've more than fifteen."

Sitting behind Partha, Bittu keeps mum. He is listening to them with keen interest.

After much persuasion Bittu was able to collect only one card. Last Monday he asked his mother for a one rupee coin but she refused straightway, "I can't give you a one rupee coin everyday to chew that trash. You must remember that the money is hard earned. It does not fall from trees." Bittu was resentful. He wanted to probe, "But how frequently do you give me money, *Ma*? You last bought me the chewing gum three months ago."

Partha has fifty gold cards which mean five hundred rupees! It's time for Bittu to get curious: how does he manage such a huge sum? He asks Partha, "Does your mother give you money every day?"

"No, only occasionally," Partha replies.

"Then how could you collect so many cards?"

Partha starts laughing, "You won't understand, stupid! This is a skill I learned from my cousin."

"Please share the trick," Bittu pleads.

"You need to pay me a fee," warns Partha. He adds, "You have to share a few cards if this scheme works."

III

Bittu gets a cut on his thumb. He fears fetching Boroline from the steel almirah, for his mother might wake up to the sound. He starts licking the finger. Saliva helps stop the bleeding, he knows. Partha has repeatedly cautioned him to wrap a piece of cloth around his finger before using the blade. Bittu cannot handle the blade even now. He uses a sharpener for pencils. The students at the art school, however, are experts in using blades. The drawing teacher once taught them how to sharpen the pencil with a blade. The pencil pointed with a sharpener does not work well for sketches, especially shades. But on every attempt he has badly lacerated fingers. Bittu gets extremely irritated and repents for not following Partha's precautionary note.

Bittu thinks it will be risky to do all of it today. Keeping things intact, he collects the earthen powder from the floor and throws it out of the window. He pays close attention to his mother. Bittu keeps an eye on her movements in the house. Each time his mother walks toward him he gets afraid. What if she finds traces of the reddish powder on the floor? He fails to concentrate on his homework. His mother scolds, finally, "What the hell is anthrologist? It is anthropologist. Have you lost it?"

Smarting over the cut Bittu inserts his thumb again in his mouth. Stopping to eat for a moment his father turns to him and asks–

"What's wrong with your finger?"

"It's cut."

"How?"

"With a blade..."

"What did you do with the blade?"

"I had to file pencils."

Sensing something wrong, Bittu's father looks at the mother apprehensively.

"I've warned you many a time not to use the blade. Why did you do it? You have sharpeners, don't you? Let me see how deep the cut is," Bittu's mother pulls his hand towards her.

"Ah! It's a minor cut. Don't worry. Finish your food; I'll dress your finger."

It's a commercial break. The Glucon D ad is being telecast on the TV. Bittu turns to his mother to find her asleep with the remote control on her chest. It's 3.30 pm. Bittu's mother would sleep for another three hours or so. Manasa*masi*, their domestic help, will come at about 5 pm. By the time she completes the chores, Bittu's mother would make tea. Bittu gets up from the bed with a strong determination: "I can't afford to miss this chance!"

Bittu brings down the Lakshmi's pot from the corner of his father's bookshelf. It is a kind of coin bank made of burnt clay. This is the pot where Bittu saves his money. Here he keeps the five-rupee-coin whenever he gets one from his father. With this money he plans to buy a carrom board during the puja vacation.

Yesterday while using the blade Bittu realized that inserting coins was way easier than taking them out through the little slit. Partha has expanded on the trick, "If the slit is made wide at least double its existing length, only then can you take out the coins using a thin broom stick."

Bittu does not need much. Only three coins will be enough. One-half plate of potato soup and a piece of loaf cost ten rupees only. He will pay Partha four rupees as fee and keep the rest for himself. Bittu has not decided what he would do with it. He starts cutting through the slit. He is careful and silent, but finds it difficult to use the blade with covered fingers. The blade frequently slips out of his grip. Bittu sweats profusely as the ceiling fan is kept idle. Each time the window curtain moves, he notices immediately. He is extremely mindful of the television sound.

"The slit looks much wider. It should not be difficult to take the coins out now," Bittu affirms himself. He lifts the earthen pot upside down. As the coins gather around the slit, Bittu pulls out just three coins with a broom stick.

IV

Bittu is in a trance. He has a vivid reverie: Ratan*da* has served him a bowl of potato soup. All the potatoes are unbroken. He hasn't seen such big, whole potatoes before. He relishes a spoonful of soup and says, "Ah! It's like the other day." Debashis once had offered him a treat when he enjoyed two spoonfuls of soup and one-half plate of potatoes. The potatoes dissolved immediately after they were taken inside the mouth. Bittu remembered the taste for a long time.

The reverie continues: Bittu is about to take another spoonful of soup, but the school-bell gongs. The break is over. Those who are playing here and there dash for their classes. Bittu tries to eat up the potatoes quickly in large gulps. But the more he eats, the more the bowl gets filled with potatoes. The sound of Utpal*babu*'s whip is circulating in the air. A piece of potato gets stuck in his throat for swallowing it hastily. His breathing chokes. Bittu starts coughing. In the dim light of the lamp, Bittu could see his mother rushing towards him with a glass of water, "*Babu*, drink this water; you are coughing badly."

V

The next morning Bittu gets ready for school a bit early. He thoroughly examines his bag to make sure that he has put the coins in the right place. While coming down the stairs, he hears the clang coming from his bag. He stands still. Seeing Bittu brake to a sudden stop, his mother asks, "What happened?"

"Nothing."

"Take care when you cross the road," his mother warns.

Bittu doesn't reply. He runs to the road. The coins clank as he walks further.

Yesterday he had put the coins in the front pocket of the schoolbag. He had no place to hide them. Very often he had to put his hand behind to make sure they were in the right place.

The clang is becoming sharper. It can be heard amidst the cacophony of the vehicles on the big road. Should Bittu hang the bag around his chest? No, it will prevent him from walking fast. It will be wise to hold the bag from behind so that it doesn't shake much.

July aunty, Bittus' next door neighbor, on her way back home from the bazaar, looks at him. She looks curious. Seeing her in front of him, Bittu lowers his eyes. He starts walking with his head down. He is afraid to raise his head. He assumes that everybody is keeping eyes on him today. The old man who reads newspapers, sitting outside the gate of the Banerjees, also appears inquisitive. It is, as if, he finds Bittu dubious... as if he could clearly see the three silvery coins. Bittu surmises that people around him would come to know about the coins: the homebound school kids, Arka*da* from their locality, and all strangers on the road.

Bittu starts running while keeping his head down. As he enters the school premises, he heads toward the classroom. Spicy aroma of the potato soup makes him stop for a while.

Keeping his hand on Bittu's shoulder, Biswajit asks, "What's wrong with you? Who's chasing you, bro?"

"Nothing like that," Bittu answers panting.

"Why did you come running then?" asks Biswajit.

"For no reason, trust me," Bittu acts smart.

Biswajit doesn't explore further. He just says, "Keep your bag; let's go to the ground for playing football."

He picks up Bittu's bag to keep it by the side of his backpack. In the twinkling of an eye Bittu jumps to him to grab it, "Don't you touch my bag!" Every day they sit together on the same bench. Biswajit is dumbfounded at Bittu's strange behavior. He looks at Bittu once again and leaves the classroom. Bittu realizes the unjust act and hits his head on the bag, "Oh God! Why did I do this? The whole world will come to know about the coins today!"

The students are singing, *Anandaloke mangalaloke birajo...* at the assembly. Amidst them, Bittu keeps looking around aimlessly. He has deliberately stood in the middle of the congregation so that none could see him. He still thinks that others are glancing at him with oblique eyes. Tapodhar stares suspiciously at him. Biswajit, standing much ahead of Bittu, looks behind to check on him. Bittu recoils gradually.

He can't grasp how everybody has understood that he has stolen fifteen rupees from his house. He notices that Amal*babu* too is observing him continually while teaching them in the classroom. Sweat gathers on Bittu's forehead. He gets dry throat. Bittu takes the three coins out of his bag during the recess and puts them inside his pocket. He goes down the stairs with a heavy heart. Joy calls him from behind, "Bittu, won't you play with us?" He shakes his head, "No."

VI

Bittu can tell that while serving potato soup to other customers, Ratan*da* keeps noticing him. For the past ten minutes he has been trying to enter Ratan*da*'s eatery but to no avail. The way Ratan*da* is keeping vigil on him suggests that he too has caught wind of it. He would perhaps call his father at night and tell him the whole thing. Bittu's hands and feet are trembling. He starts walking to his home.

His hand inserted in the pocket becomes wet with sweat. He feels like bursting into tears. Bittu remembers the day when a thief was caught in their locality and tied to the lamppost. Several people from his neighbourhood gathered to see the thief. Bittu feels even more restless. Tears roll down his cheeks. Bittu tries hard to muster up strength. Wiping his tears, he enters the home to find his mother doing her hair. She asks, "*Babu*, are you hungry? Shall I make *ruti* for you?"

"I won't eat," Bittu gives a sharp reply.

Taking off the school uniform he lies down in the bed.

"Aren't you hungry?" Bittu's mother asks again.

"I don't feel like eating *ruti* now, *Ma*," Bittu responds.

"What happened? Are you okay?" she inquires.

She puts her hand affectionately on Bittu's forehead. "I'm fine!" Bittu feels disturbed and turns to the other side of the bed. His mother lies down beside him.

It's time for the second commercial break of the daily soap, *Happy Family*. Bittu fails to sleep. However, his mother falls asleep within a few minutes and starts snoring. Bittu stands up on the bed and takes down the Lakshmi's pot down carefully. He takes the coins from his bag and inserts them into the pot. He keeps it in the right place.

The sky appears overcast with cloud, tantalizing with rain. The south-wind blows. Bittu quickly climbs up the stairs to the roof. The wind has gained momentum; dry leaves are covering the whole roof. The trees are slanting madly. He watches a whirlpool of dust as it covers the road.

"Bittu, come down now. There is tremendous flash of lightning!"

"I'm enjoying the wind." Bittu says aloud.

"No, never! Come down right now." Bittu's mother warns.

Bathed in dust Bittu comes down the stairs at breakneck speed and tightly hugs his mother, "*Ma, Ma,* give me something to eat. I'm so hungry!"

BROKEN MOON

The train slows down before pulling into Sealdah station. Leaving her seat, Pritha walks toward the gate and stands there, firmly gripping the handle. Blown by the air, her torn *dupatta* entangles around the vertical iron rod fixed in the middle of the gateway. Pritha lets it remain coiled until she gets off.

It's a full moon tonight. The soft moonlight seeps through the chinks of the tin shade that makes a canopy over the platform. Pritha comes out of the station. Tonight, owing to the full moon, her *Baba* probably won't turn on the lamps in the yard. He might light them in case the sky is cloudy. And then, a deluge of fluorescence will inundate the garden, making every inch of it as bright as daylight. Darkness will, however, reign supreme inside the house. After retirement this yard has become Arpan's only area of dwelling.

I

Pritha can vividly remember what happened on the last day at his school. It was late evening and Arpan wasn't home by then. Maya, Pritha's mother, was on tenterhooks. Without losing her cool, Pritha, urged: "Stop worrying, *Ma. Baba* isn't a child."

"But isn't it too late?"

"*Ma*, it's his last day at school, where he taught for a good thirty-two years!"

"This makes no sense."

"Be practical, *Ma*. Is it really easy to sever all the bonding *Baba* has grown over the years with his colleagues, students and the school itself? Besides, the students will throw a farewell party for sure. Have patience, he will be back soon."

Arpan returned around eight o'clock with some packets of sweets, one shawl, an umbrella, and two full bags of fruits.

While unpacking the gifts, Pritha inquired, "*Baba*, didn't they give you a memento?"

Arpan hid something behind his apparent smile. "You should have returned home early," Maya said resentfully.

"Maya, the farewell ceremony ended only an hour ago." Arpan replied emptying a glass of water in one swallow.

Arpan, however, retired not only from his service but from life at large. He cocooned himself in his own world that only comprised of his house and the garden. Although his colleagues phoned him on and off, Arpan didn't show interest to welcoming them home. Gradually, they stopped keeping in touch.

Kamal, Pritha's classmate and a neighbor, was a student of Arpan. Still he never addressed him "Sir." He called him *Kaku*. Arpan himself, however, didn't have the teacher-cum-guardian like airs at home. Neither did he talk much. When in class, he had never discussed anything beyond the texts. His students knew that very well. Arpan never enjoyed providing tuition to students individually in home. Kamal's father approached him quite a few times, "Sir, would you please teach Kamal separately on a one-to-one basis?" Arpan declined but suggested a remedy, "You can ask Kamal to come to the teachers' room. I shall be there and take care of his studies."

Arpan and Maya shared a warm relationship throughout. However, Maya always had her share of complaints: "Have you ever thought of our future? Do you have any idea about the money we need for Pritha's wedding? An average reception will cost you approximately five lacs. What is even worse, in case one of us falls ill, we will be in a trying predicament as the treatment in any medical institution is too expensive to afford, and we don't have medical insurance either. What's wrong with teaching students privately at home?"

Maya continued: "Look at Basanta. He is ten years junior to you in service. He owns two houses and a car, banking only on private tuitions. He flies off to Vellore every time he falls sick.

And think of us—we shy away from senior consultants who charge more than the junior practitioners."

Arpan would keep mum. But, this didn't stop Maya from carrying on: "Well, tell me something. How can you explain that you are bankrupt after spending money for the two-storey house we live in? You were in a government job for a long time. Yet you fall short of funds for your only daughter's wedding. We will simply die in a hospital without treatment if we fall ill, for we don't have enough money."

Maya, of course, did not allow him the chance for her to be hospitalized. It was drizzling since dawn. An early riser Maya did not wake up even after Pritha had left the bed that day. Pritha thought her mother was sleeping more than usual owing to the soothing weather. But after making tea when she went to rouse her from sleep, she found Maya as cold as ice.

Arpan used to slip into the garden without disturbing Maya. In the morning he would look after the flower plants and other saplings. Even the foulest weather could not deter him from his daily activities in the front yard.

Hearing Pritha scream in despair, Arpan ran up to her and without wasting time called up a doctor. When the doctor handed him the death certificate, he stood still for quite some time. After reading the certificate thoroughly, he asked Pritha, "Will you perform the rituals and set her face on fire?" Offering a few hundred bucks, he advised his brother-in-law to arrange for Maya's final journey. But Arpan didn't even touch his wife. He did not mourn or sit by her side for the last time either. In the burning ghat he touched her mouth with the last morsel of cooked rice. He blew off the flame of the burning jute sticks, perhaps to prevent her from being scorched.

During the next fortnight the house was full. The aunts and uncles stayed there by rotation. Kamal came twice a day. While talking to Kamal in her room, Pritha failed to hold her tears back. Having pressed her hands, Kamal said, "Please don't lose your heart. I'll be with you, always."

Pritha flopped down on Kamal's chest, counting him to be the only pillar of support. In fact, none of them ever proposed to each other. They grew up together. In their childhood days Kamal and his friends deliberately disturbed Pritha in the outdoor games and made fun of her. Pritha used to retaliate through pranks, calling Kamal a banana-loving ape. After passing the school leaving exam, they both enrolled for Samanta*babu*'s tutorial with the focus of majoring in Geography. The classes generally ended late in the evenings, the lanes were dark as there were no street lamps. It was Arpan who used to accompany Pritha on her way back home. Kamal had suggested, "Why don't you tell *Kaku* that he need not come? I'm here, and since I stay so close to your house, I can always take you along."

"No point, Kamal. Come he must," said Pritha while marking the Chilkalake with a pencil.

One day Arpan had high fever and could not make it to fetch her. Kamal had led Pritha to her house. It was the first time that Pritha blushed. She thought of how their neighbors had taken it. And this was when Kamal had felt the first pulse of his manhood.

After a few days, however, things returned to normal and the memory blurred as they had the chance of talking freely in the college premises, and on their way back home. They never felt like proposing to each other, or celebrating a romantic Valentine's Day though they could have done that easily. Pritha could have held his hand without any hesitation. And even when she was fooled by her friends, she didn't procrastinate to say, "Yes, Kamal is my boyfriend." On hearing this Kamal was curious, "Oh my my! Did you really say that?" These days, nevertheless, they don't have enough time to indulge in frequent conversations.

Soon after Maya's death, Arpan gradually withdrew himself from everything and started spending more time in the garden. He himself arranged the yard with soft white lamps. Sitting on a cane chair at the nightfall he used to switch on these lamps. The glare mixed with the soothing moonlight looked celestial. Arpan sat in here until late at night. Pritha used to observe him through the window of her first floor room. In fact, when she first noticed him in the garden, she was scared.

Kamal came to see Pritha two months ago. He was busy with the ward councilor Nag*babu*.

Looking forward to his favor for the settlement of a civic volunteer's job he ran errands for him. Since Kamal's father was about to retire in October, he didn't object to Kamal's hanging around political connections in the locality. Kamal passed his Bachelors with a poor second class. Of course, he wouldn't have done post graduation had he obtained a first. Pritha wanted to convince him, "Please complete at least an online Masters."

"What good will that do?" Kamal asked. "There's no update on a government teaching job for the last four years. And even if you do Masters there's no job in the private sector either."

Kamal did not even provide tuitions to students, ignoring his mother's repeated persuasions, "See, how, in spite of being a girl, Pritha moves around teaching students. And you?"

"Leave it, *Ma*. You know, providing tuitions is worse than begging on the streets. Ask Pritha to know how much she earns, and how difficult it is to collect the fees from the students."

So, giving up all the hopes of being a teacher Kamal became an ardent follower of Nag*babu*, the secretary of the local club and councilor. Those who helped him in the election had been offered the temporary job of a civic volunteer. Kamal, thus, became a party member.

Pritha laughed at his waving the party flag: "I've never seen you do politics in the college. And now you are walking in a political rally with a party flag!"

Kamal pulled up a cushion and reclined on it. He addressed Pritha's concern, "You won't understand. There is a saying in Hindi— *Waqt aane pe gadhe ko bhi baap banana padta hai* (when needed, you have to consider a sheep your father.)."

"Shut up! You could have enrolled for the Masters, rather. Remember, you will age with every passing day."

"Oh! I see. You are getting late, darling. I'm sure there are several prospective grooms who are waiting in the queue. Your Bubu*masi* is indeed a reliable media."

Pritha refrained from passing a remark.

Pritha can remember one day *Ma* was diagnosed with high blood pressure. She had a reeling head. Finally, a female cook, Bubu, was commissioned. She was in her mid-forties. She lived in a slum near the EM Bypass, Garia. Bubu had a small plot of land close to the main road. Her husband was a drunkard who was run over after fifteen years of their marriage. During the construction of the expressway, her in-laws managed to sell the land to a developer, faking Bubu's signature. But they didn't pay her anything, not even a shilling. One fine morning a bulldozer smashed her house. Bubu could barely save her belongings. She had to live by the side of the main road with her fourteen-year-old daughter, Sona. Slowly, Bubu and her daughter settled in a hut in that slum area. But they were not safe there either. Recently the government notified them to quit the place. A statue of Subhas Chandra Bose would be built there. The local contractor Bhola*da* got the tender.

Since that time Bubu and her daughter were spending sleepless nights because of the fear of being homeless. What was more, Sona's school leaving examination was ahead. So Bubu had to work very hard to bear the expenses of her education and to eke out a living for them. She worked in two more families. She also doubled up as Pritha's personal assistant and a reliable companion, helping her in every step. However, she and her daughter spent most of the time in Pritha's house. This saved on their dinner and Sona's additional expenses for English and Maths tuition. But that was not the reason why Bubu was eager to look out for prospective grooms for Pritha. She stood very humbly before Arpan, though he would never talk to her with a raised voice, let alone give her a rebuff.

"Can I tell you something, *babu*?"

Arpan was putting the right amount of manure in some small paper packets for the saplings he planted in the garden.

"Say."

"*Babu*, could you please look at this photo? He is a nice gentleman, a government servant. He owns a house in Naihati. His mobile number is written on the back of the picture."

"Okay." Arpan did not say more. He won't, perhaps, open the envelope that had the photo inside. It would lie on the table for a few days. And then it would invariably mingle with the heap of scraps and old newspapers to be sold at a throw-away price. Bubu was aware of this. Yet, she would get hold of a new photo every other day.

Arpan turned into silence incarnate. After Maya's demise, Pritha tried hard to be very friendly with her father. "Well, you can always ask Bubu*masi* not to bring the photos?" Arpan smiled and dropped the envelope in the paper basket. Pritha put on an air of affected chagrin at this. Arpan covered up everything under his smile, as usual.

"*Baba*, why do you light up all those lamps in the garden?"

After a long pause Arpan replied, "I prefer soft lighting. I find the dazzling ones repulsive. All these years my employer paid me for illumining the tender minds of the students. And now I light the lamps just for me. There is no remuneration."

Pritha sat down for a while. She tried to understand what Arpan said. And then she went up, turning off all the lights downstairs. Arpan took up a chair to sit down in the yard that overflowed with moonlight.

II

Arpan never bothered to check who entered the house. He remained busy with the plants and lamps in the courtyard. He became a ludicrous figure to his neighbors. People used to call him by funny names. Kamal was ashamed of this and he rarely walked the road that led to

Pritha's house. And Pritha was a free soul. She always followed her heart. She used to return home around 11 pm from Garia where she taught a few students. Kamal didn't appreciate her being so late and requested her many a time to quit the tuition class.

Pritha was prompt in addressing him, "You have a mentor, but I don't have a Nag*babu* who will get me a job."

There was another concern: Pritha turned a rebel all of a sudden. She didn't want to give up the fight for Bubu who was desperate to hold on to the hut she lived in. But Kamal insisted to Pritha: "I'm telling you to stay away from this issue."

"But why?"

"You are being suicidal, Pritha!"

"Is this a threat?"

"No. Why would you call it a threat? Listen, the guys who will now come won't simply limit themselves to threatening you. They won't offer you a bouquet of flowers either as you are my girlfriend."

"Had I been your girlfriend, you couldn't have said this. Tell your boss to do whatever he wants. I'm not going to call it quits."

Pulling up a chair, Kamal flopped down on it. He came to see her after four months: "It's so difficult to make you understand my point. Why are you hell-bent on risking your life for the sake of the maid? If you like her donate money and get rid of the trouble."

Kamal nibbled at his nail: "Last evening Nag*babu* called me to the club to say, "Listen, here is a task for you, but maintain privacy and security. I know it's your family matter. I have convinced Bhola*da* to hold his plans for a while. You are well aware of what happens if he involves himself in this issue.""

Bhola*da* was the zonal secretary, a millionaire owing to his real estate business. He had magical skills to build up high risers even in the most disputed land. He was equally rich in manpower.

"Pritha, please think over it one last time. Afterward this will be beyond my control." Finishing the tea, Kamal put the cup down on the table. Pritha was brushing her hair facing the window. She answered, "I'll also ask you to give it a second thought. If they don't set up the statue there, there will be no loss. But the survival of those poor dwellers will be impaired."

Scraping out the coiled hairs from the hairbrush, Pritha threw them into the bin and Kamal took French leave.

For the last few months Pritha came across Kamal only on the roads, especially during nighttime on her way back home. She found him freaking out with other party members near the Sitala temple. Kamal used to come forward and accompany her up to a certain distance and then they parted ways. If and when Kamal phoned Pritha she made sure it was urgent, otherwise she would ask him to call again later in the night. Six years passed and Kamal developed the habit of keeping alone.

Pritha observed that people found loneliness attractive, and distance could actually bridge the gap between two or more human beings. There were relationships that broke as well. Being alone made one probe a relationship better.

While leaving for home in the evening Bubu urged Pritha, "*Didi*, I won't come tomorrow for work. Please take care of the chores."

"Why? Where would you go?"

"I will visit the police station again and a few government officials for this issue. But I fear the worst. I anticipate that you will be affected for standing by us. Nag*babu* and his folks are not good men."

"Oh! Don't worry. Leave it to me and relax. Tomorrow I've plans to visit some media offices. So don't be absent."

"Please, *Didi*. Let me take a day's leave. From the day after tomorrow I'll be regular," Bubu asked Pritha, holding her hands with much love and gratitude. Pritha let her leave without insisting.

After being forgetful for some time Pritha remembered that she was getting late. So she went to the dining table and arranged plates for lunch. She knew that neither Bubu nor her daughter would have lunch at their house today. She called her father, who was sitting silent. Bubu would be trying hard this time to save the plot of land where she lived with her daughter. Yesterday Pritha accompanied Bubu to the police station and to Nag*babu* and his associates. Bubu submitted her appeal in writing to all of them but to no avail. Rather Pritha had to stomach much insult.

The police officer told Pritha, "They have forcefully occupied the government's land and don't want to vacate the area even after receiving repeated notifications. Listen, intellectuals like you create major problems for the progress of the nation." The police officer didn't bother to read Bubu's appeal. On the other hand, being thorough with what Bubu wrote in her letter, Nag*babu* addressed Pritha in a grave voice, "They are not evacuees, they had the land, and during the construction of the highway they got proper compensation from the government. All her signed papers are lying with the authority. What wrong are we doing? If she squanders away the entire money she received, what can we do? And those who are opposing the building of the statue and the developmental work are actually on the illegal side. So, please don't involve yourself in this dispute or you too will find troubles."

"Won't Bubu and her daughter have lunch today?" asked Arpan.

"No, they won't come today. Bubu*masi* will visit a few administrative officers."

Pritha put two boiled potatoes, a pinch of salt, half teaspoonful of mustard oil and some slices of onion in a bowl. She mashed them all. Taking a scoop of the dough, she put it on his plate.

"Ask Bubu to stay on the ground floor with her daughter, if she wishes so. Don't worry about me. I'll sleep upstairs," said Arpan.

While serving rice, Pritha looked at him. Arpan fished out the chilies from the lentil soup and put them aside. Pritha quickly finished her lunch and went out.

The next day Pritha woke up early in the morning and started working according to her plans. She posted an update on Facebook. It was shared by thirteen users within a short span of time. Many had sent her messages, "We are with you."

Pritha knew all these virtual supports would be of no real use. However, she believed that on this lonely planet all such messages would reinforce her moral strength.

III

Visiting the television broadcast center when Pritha boarded the train, it was quite late. As the train was nearing Park Circus, her cell phone rang. "Is it *Baba*?" But Arpan hardly phoned her without a reason.

Taking the phone out of her purse Pritha found that the journalist, Saugato Malakar, was calling. Yesterday she got a chance to meet him in the media office. Saugato listened to all that she had to say and gave her his phone number: "Keep me posted. Don't hesitate to inform me when you face any problem."

So, as the goons got down at Ballygunj station, Pritha rang Saugato first. But he did not take the call.

"Oh Pritha, sorry I was outside, say."

"Saugato*da*, today I've been threatened by some hooligans."

"Where did they board the train?" Saugato asked.

"I didn't really notice. But the moment the train left Dhakuria they flanked me in the coach that was quite empty."

"Do you know them?"

"Yes, they are Kamal's friends. Two of them were my father's students."

"And then?

"I'm shocked. They somehow got to know of my visit to the media houses. At first they scolded me in uncouth language and also asked me to delete my Facebook post. As I refused to follow, they started slapping and blowing me at random. They tore my *dupatta* by dragging me," Pritha got a choked throat.

"Have you thought of reporting the incident to the police?"

"I can't decide, Saugato*da*. Please suggest a way out."

"Look, it's difficult to make any suggestion in such critical matters as I won't be able to give you security if something worse happens. Don't misunderstand me, Pritha. Today they have insulted you, abused you, torn your clothes, because they know you. They wanted to warn you in a big way so that you don't proceed further in this matter. Am I right?"

"Yes, you are."

"If something graver happens tomorrow, I can only arrange for two or three talk shows. But after that the city will lapse into fruitless political struggles. Do remember that even for a candle walk one needs to possess good luck."

Pritha understood what Saugato meant. He knew what was what. She kept silent.

Trains don't usually halt so long before entering Sealdah station from Park Circus. Today it's been quite a while. There is a handful of passengers on the platform. A few drunkards are resting here and there, forming queer geometrical shapes. Some vagabonds are trudging along the platform. Pritha looks at the big digital clock hung on the wall. It is a quarter past eleven. She starts walking faster. Those few people on the platform look at Pritha with wide eyes. She tries to hide the torn part of the *dupatta* that hangs from her left shoulder. Before alighting from the train, she has seen her face on the front camera of her mobile phone. She has noticed the finger marks on her face. Pritha will show her torn *dupatta* to Kamal in case she finds him at Sitalatala. She decides to wear the same dress while staging *dharna* before the crushed hut of Bubu.

Kamal is sitting at Sitalatala all alone tonight. Seeing him Pritha takes off her torn *dupatta*. Kamal keeps looking at her bluntly, tightening his jaws. He doesn't stand up to walk toward her. Pritha slowly walks past him toward her house with a heavy heart. Entering the gate she notices that despite the full-moon Arpan has switched on all the lamps in the garden. Pritha locks the front gate and stands there looking at the lights. It appears that all the moonbeams of the universe have stood thronging in the yard. Sitting on the porch Arpan looks at Pritha. She takes off her shoes.

Notifications on her last Facebook update keep popping up on the phone. On her way back home she has written a post asking for public opinion: *Netaji, you never believed in statues. Please don't evacuate us from here.*

From tomorrow Pritha will be staging *dharna* before Bubu's hut. Pulling a cane chair near him Pritha sits and asks her father, "It's full moon, why have you turned on all the lamps, *Baba*?"

Arpan does not bother to look at his daughter. He responds, "I felt like lighting up the garden tonight. There is so much darkness around which the full moon fails to eliminate. I can't see even myself."

"How can you see, *Baba*? How long will you help the darkness with this artificial light?"

Arpan laughs at Pritha's words. Pritha feels irritated. Her eyes get blurry. There is a hatch by the side of the door. Before going to sleep Arpan shuts the door with it. Maya did the same when she was alive. Pritha goes and picks up the big hatch. She enters straight into the garden and with it starts hitting hard on the lamps. Arpan is clueless as to what's happening. He shouts, "What the hell are you doing? Stop it, Pritha."

The lamps are dying out one by one. Amidst the noise of shattering of the glass, a groan is heard. Arpan understands it's Pritha who is sobbing. As the last filament is dashed into pieces, a sort of mysterious darkness descends to engulf the entire garden amid the full moon night.

Pritha throws away the hatch and sits on the porch with a heavy thud. The full moonlight diffuses across the porch, revealing the chiaroscuro of nature. Amidst that eerie atmosphere they look like two shadowy figures. After some time Pritha breaks the lull: "*Baba*, don't you try to restore the lamps to lighten them again. You have no right to do that now. But it is you who could have enlightened a thousand young minds. You had the scope and capability, but you failed." Uttering all these in quick succession, Pritha takes a deep breath and sinks into silence.

Critical Acclaim for Bitan Chakraborty

Life is a spectrum of contrasting colors and feelings, of blacks & whites, of light and darkness, and the art of opposites is a necessary mechanism which refines the sensibilities of an artist to arrive at a realization, so aptly demonstrated by Chakraborty. *—Theatre Street Journal* (March, 2019)

Mr. Chakraborty writes not about the elites of India's society, not about the beautiful people of Bollywood fantasies. He brings to life the small and all too ordinary tales of common people. His characters are not always likeable but always real to life. We know them. We can identify with them. They move through a world where everyone else is also struggling to get by. Everyone is grubbing and grasping. Everyone is on the fiddle; everyone is extending a palm to be greased. *—Red Fez Magazine* (Issue 90)

Chakraborty expertly weaves the city into the story and the effect is seamless. Chakraborty gracefully avoids one of the biggest stumbling blocks that the short story writers trip on these days. Each sentence, each sight earns its place in the story. Many characters are sketched out with such care that they could be your next door neighbor or the beggar woman with whom you often avoid eye contact at a traffic signal. These characters reveal their stories, their trials and turbulence, their possible realities through Chakraborty's evocative portraiture. *—Literature Studio Review* (October 2016)

Bitan Chakraborty

Bitan Chakraborty is best known as the founder of *Hawakal Publishers*. He is also an acclaimed story writer, translator, and editor of the Bengali print journal, *Atibhuj*. Heading one of the foremost independent presses in India, Chakraborty has finally been bestowed the title as one of "the flag-bearers of verse" in Indian subcontinent. As a proficient raconteur, Chakraborty has made a lasting impact with his collection of Bengali short fiction, *Santiram-er Cha*, which was later translated into English under the title, *Bougainvillea and Other Short Stories*. Having authored six collections of prose and poetry, Bitan Chakraborty emerges as an extremely talented littérateur of the present day.

More at www.bitanchakraborty.com

Utpal Chakraborty

A teacher of English literature, translator, author of academic interest and bilingual poet Utpal Chakraborty is a regular contributor to leading Bengali and English magazines, including *Desh*, *Kabisammelan*, *Abahaman*, *Pratidin*, *Contour*, *Mad Swirl*, *Tuck Magazine*, *Scarlet Leaf Review*, among other places. His *Concept*, containing critical appreciations of prose and poetry, and his books on writing skill released by the Kolkata based *Nabodaya Publications* have been well received by the teachers and the taught alike. Utpal's *Uranta Dolphin*, an acclaimed collection of fifty-five Bengali poems, has been published by *Signet Press*.